KAMA-SUTRA
OF
VATSYAYANA

The Art of Lovemaking

Translated and edited by
Mishul Das

TABLE OF CONTENTS

TABLE OF CONTENTS

TABLE OF CONTENTS

TABLE OF CONTENTS

INTRODUCTION

No finer tribute has perhaps been paid to the personality and of Vatsyayana than that paid by Sir Richard Burton, the eminent Orientalist, who had delved deep into the ancient literature on the East and the West:

"The works of men of genius do follow them and remain as a lasting treasure. And thong): there may be disputes and discussions about the immortality of the body or the soul, nobody can deny the immortality of genius, which ever remains as a bright and guiding star to the struggling humanities of the succeeding ages. This work (the KAMA-SUTRA), then, which has stood the test of centuries, has placed Vatsyayana among the immortals, and on this, and on him no better elegy or eulogy can be written than the following lines :

"So long as lips shall kiss, and eyes shall see,

So long lives this, and This gives life to Thee."

Yet there are few men who share the enthusiasm and praise of Sir Richard Burton. Many people in India are familiar with the name of Vatsyayana and his KAMA-SUTRA, but there is a wide spread ignorance about what he actually wrote. Not a few educated men regard the work as a fantastic or pornographic work on the abnormalities of sexual behaviour. This is very deplorable but not quite inexplicable. For Vatsyayana wrote in a language that ceased to be spoken centuries ago ; correct renderings of the KAMA-SUTRA in the current languages are few and not easily available and much of the literature that claims to be renderings or adaptations of the KAMA-SUTRA has little actual relation to the book and is full of fanciful, sometimes unwholesome, descriptions of sexual behaviour borrowed from well-known foreign writers on sex.

The KAMA-SUTRA presents a complete and objective picture of the sexual life of Vatsyayana's times, when society had settled down to a feudal order of existence and a hereditary leisured class had developed a highly sophisticated manner of living in urban areas. Polygamy was common and the courtesan had become an integral part of the social life of the town. Early marriage of girls through family negotiation was becoming more and more general, but in many urban areas girls grew up as virgins and, there being considerable freedom of movement for women, contracted love marriages within or without the same social set.

The literature of the period also affords instances of courtesans marrying respectable citizens. Re-marriage of widows was not yet prohibited, though moral recognition of such marriages was almost withheld. Wealth and vigour combined to make men seek the society of several wives, concubines and courtesans for the satisfaction of their desires that were as much the product of the sexual impulse as of education and artistic training. On the other hand, it provided wives with a large field for dissatisfaction. Many of them were tied to one husband who in many Cases had to meet the sexual demands of several women. A respectable women therefore, had the choice of two courses: to excel in the art of monopolizing the husband's love, or to seek solace in the arms of a clandestine lover.

The outlook disclosed by Vatsyayana in the treatment of the sexual passion is amazingly sane and modern. He has open partiality for love marriages among grown up men and women and for monogamous domestic life. He shows women how to qualify for meeting all the love demands of a normal sexed husband, which include sexual and, no less equally sentimental and cultural factors, o that she may escape the curse of being saddled with a rival. That is why he insists that women should learn, as well as men, the sixty-four cultural arts.

He also stresses that love does not alone solve the problem of sexual relationship and that physical and passional disparities have no less to be reckoned with. A modicum of love between husband and wife may be presumed to exist in the average case, but these disparities and ignorance of the ways of ironing them out have made homes unhappy and caused trouble and distress in all ages. Vatsyayana has discussed this problem and suggested remedies for it in a scientific manner and with a detachment that have not yet been excelled. He is the world's pioneer and first authoritative exponent of systematic sex education, which he holds is the best and most practical method of self-control and happiness.

Vatsyayana has sometimes been criticized disparagingly for his minute descriptions of intimate sexual conduct and for describing the sexual customs, sometimes revolting, of different localities. Such critics, of course, accept certain pragmatic and essentially personal Ideas about sexual morality as immutable standards by which to judge the question of sex. They would not make allowances for differences in moral standards in view of differences social conditions, place and time, nor would they permit them selves even to think that humanity represents many different types that are very differently endowed with the libidinous passion. To a student who has made a careful study of the conditions of feudal society in the different countries in different ages, it will appear that certain vices or excesses were inherent in the very composition of the feudal order, where the male of the species among the leisured or ruling classes had enough power in his hands to draw up a special moral code for their own class. The description of the ways of seducing others wives, for example. leaves no doubt in the reader's mind that this vice was mostly confined among the royalty and within the court circles. . Let this picture be compared to those of Italian and French aristocracy of the Middle Ages, and a family resemblance will at once be noticed.

And what about the present age? Substitute "plutocracy" for aristocracy and the picture will be very similar in its broad outlines.

The objection relating to the minutiæ of intimate behaviour is simply due to prudery and ignorance. Vatsyayana had realised that sexual satisfaction in woman was as important as in man. He even goes so far as to warn his readers that without sexual satisfaction a woman's physical and mental constitution may be come unbalanced. As has already been noted, physical and passional disparities make complete mutual satisfaction difficult of attainment, and the careful reader will note how helpful Vatsyayana has been to the husband who may have anxieties on that score. Almost all that Vatsyayana has said about love-play, etc., has been amply corroborated by modern medical literature on sex. It is rather amazing that the treatment of this matter in some of the most reputed and up-to-date works on sex is exactly on the lines of the KAMA-SUTRA. Of course, modern writers have the advantage in that they know more about the anatomy and physiology of sex than did our ancient sage. But neither in the matter of psychology of passion nor in that of ways and means does Vatsyayana yield place to such famous authors as Van de Velde or even Iwan Bloch. The home and the world would certainly be happier for young men and women if they understood the rationale and technique of passion, a complex biological-cum cultural necessity of the present day.

Vatsyayana has written his invaluable work in Sanskrit aphorisms that are sometimes brief to the point of obscurity. Like many other Sutras on other subjects some of them are capable, on the face of them, of different interpretations. The rational way of understanding their true implications is to refer constantly to the commentary called JAYAMANGALA, reputedly by Yashodhara, which has been accepted for centuries as the correct annotation to the KAMA-SUTRA.

Care has been taken to present the work, as accurately as possible, in simple modern English. Nothing has been stated in the body of the work that does not occur in the KAMA-SUTRA, all explanatory or commentative remarks furnished by the editors being introduced as footnotes to distinguish them from the textual rendering. The standard Benares texts of the Sutras and the commentary have been followed but the arrangement of the chapters has been somewhat altered in view of the requirements and tastes of present-day readers, The editors realise that this is a big liberty taken by them, for Vatsyayana was nothing if not a master of method.

In conclusion, the editors beg to state that it has been their aim to produce an entirely new edition of the KAMA-SUTRA, of the essential sobriety and utility of which they are so convinced that they have no hesitation in recommending this book to all men and women who have entered, or are about to enter, the married state. They regret that the unsettled conditions of the present time have interfered with the preparation of this book.

CHAPTER 1
THE ORIGINS OF THE KAMASUTRA

VATSYAVANA begins by acknowledging the objectives of life-dharma (religion and morality), artha (wealth and material prosperity) and kama (pleasure), for these are also the ultimate objectives of all the Scriptures!. He pays his respects to those preceptors Old who have made deep studies in these things and have instructed others. The present work is intimately related to the experiences and teachings of those great men, it being a selection from, and condensation of, their several works.

It has been authoritatively stated that after having created animals and human beings upon the earth, the Lord of Creation gave instructions, for their progress and preservation, in the method of achievement of the three objectives, in one hundred thousand chapters. The Swayambhuva Manu (the law-giver of the Hindus), who was self-born, took out from that vast body of instructions the part dealing with dharma and compiled a treatise laying down the principles of religion and morality. Vrihaspati dealt with another part and made up a treatise on the Science of Wealth. Nandi, the follower of Mahadeva, took out still another part and compiled, in one thousand chapters, a treatise on the Science of Love. He was the father of Sexual Science. Svetaketu, son of Uddalaka, later condensed this work into five hundred chapters. Vabhravya, a native of Panchala State (the Ganges-Jumna doab south of Delhi), further condensed it into one hundred and fifty chapters under the following seven divisions :

(1) General considerations;

(2) Concerning virgin brides;

(3) Concerning wives;

(4) Concerning prostitutes;

(5) Concerning mistresses who may be wives of others;

(6) Concerning the technique of sexual union of men and women, and

(7) Secret instructions (on aphrodisiacs, art of beautification etc.).

Dattaka wrote a monograph on the division concerning the art and technique of prostitutes at the request of the courtesans of Pataliputra city (modern Patna.), the capital of the Magadha empire. Similarly, Charayana dealt separately with the division General considerations and incorporated in it the results of his own researches. Ghotakamukha dealt with the division relating to young wives: Gonardiva with that relating to sexually experienced wives: Gonikaputra with that relating to mistresses: Suvarnanabha with that relating to the technique of sexual union and Kuchumara with the secret instructions. As a result of such partial treatment by many preceptors the culture of the science of sex as a whole received little attention.

People consulted the particular division which they might be interested, and as no one felt the urge to study the sexual science comprehensively, the mass of knowledge handed down from Nandi to Vabhravya was threatened with complete oblivion. In view of this and the facts that the works of Dattaka and others are concerned with particular aspects of the science and that Vabhravya's authoritative treatise is too voluminous to be read with comfort, Vatsyayana condenses the treatment of all the divisions into this Kama-sutra or Principles of the Science of Sexual Passion"—an abstract of the whole of the works of the above-named authors within a small compass.

CHAPTER 2
RELATIVE IMPORTANCE OF DHARMA, ARTHA AND KAMA

MAN and woman have a hundred-year cycle of life. This should be so divided as to offer the harmonious and coordinated pursuit of the three objectives of life: the acquisition of religious merit and Wealth and the satisfaction of love-desires.

There are three stages of life- (i) child (ii) manhood and iii) old age. One is a child up to the age of sixteen, a man up to the age of seventy, and an old man from seventy upwards. Childhood should be devoted to education, manhood to the acquisition of Wealth and satisfaction of amorous passion and old age to the acquisition of merit and release from bondage to the recurring cycle of birth and death.

In real life, however, it is not possible to confine the pursuit of the three objectives to the three different stages. In receiving his education, for example, a boy is not only acquiring merit by doing his duty. but is also preparing himself for the pursuit of wealth and for the proper exercise of his passions. Further, in taking a wife, a man may be doing his duty as well as procuring an instrument for the exercise of his passion. Even in the act of sexual union, a man, while satisfying his love-desire, may be acting in the furtherance of his task of begetting progeny, which is enjoined by the Scriptures. Again, considering the uncertainty of life, he should pursue, at whatever period possible, whichever objective he considers proper. One thing, however, is strictly enjoined: one must exercise the strictest continence so long as one is a student.

There are certain actions, as for instance, the taking of meat and other things, which arise out of our instinctive desires.

These are universal because their effects, such as the satisfaction of hunger and the consequent feeling of well-being, are readily observed.

But rituals, sacrifices and expiatory actions prescribed by the Holy Books (Shastras) are not popularly observed, for their effects are intangible to the senses. When one defers to the commands of the Holy Books, dutifully observes the rules of rituals, sacrifices etc., and refrains from unrestricted partaking of meat, purposeless killing of animals, theft of others' property, incest, adultery. fornication and the drinking of unconsecrated liquor, such restraint is called dharma or piety. Instructions in such piety should be had from Books or from a college of competent preceptors.

The acquisition of knowledge, landed property, precious metals, horses, elephants, cows and other cattle, food crops like rice etc., utensils and furniture made of metal, wood, earthen ware and leather, friends, garments and ornaments and the increment of what one possesses or has acquired constitute what is meant by artha or wealth. Instructions in the pursuit of wealth should be obtained from officers of State whom it is customary for kings to appoint those to be in charge of different departments of the administration, or from experts in such occupations as agriculture etc., or from people engaged in commerce.

The desire for pleasurable experience through the five senses-hearing, touch, sight, taste and smell—under the Significance of guidance of the mind which is inseparably connected with the Ego (atma) is called kama in its general significance. The object of. this desire is to obtain pleasure. But the special sense in which the word kama has been used throughout the Kamasutra is denoted by that powerful desire felt by men and women for a particular contact which produces the maximum pleasure, attended by other minor pleasures which are like shadows in comparison with the greater pleasure. By this definition, the significance of kama (libido sexualis) has been narrowed down to the urge for that extreme pleasure which comes to man and woman through their respective genital organs coming into contact during coital movement.

The necessary acts-touching, kissing, embracing, titillating etc. have been relegated to the position of secondary, in fact, apparent or minor pleasures. One should be educated in the art of love by studying the Kama-sutra or by attending soirées and meetings of citizens well experienced in the art. Should one find it necessary to pursue the three objectives (religious merit. wealth and satisfaction of erotic desire) at the same time, one should select the one that is the most important. For example, satisfaction of erotic desire is subordinate to pursuit of wealth, which, again, is subordinate to that of religious merit. Religious merit, therefore, has the pride of place among des objectives. This, however, does not hold true for every body, for to a king wealth is the more important; since his way of life is indissolubly bound up with wealth. Again, wealth being the occupation of public women, they should prefer it to the other two.

Dharma is not a widely understood objective and only the Sacred Books can set forth the technique of achieving it. To get the best results out of anything, one should adopt the best method of doing it. Both in the acquisition of dharma and artha it is in the authoritative works on the respective subjects that the best method can be found. But erotic passion or karma reigns in every creature: it occurs spontaneously not only in man but also in animals. Some preceptors are, therefore, of the opinion that there is no need of education in Sexual Science. The answer to this objection is that passion in man and woman, whether in the general or in the special sense, is dependent for its satisfaction upon certain steps being taken by them. The knowledge of these may come from a study of the Kama Shastra. The non-application of proper means, which we observe in the brute creation, is caused by their being unrestrained and by the female of the species being fit for sexual intercourse only when in rut, and that, too, in order to conceive. Again, this urge is instinctive and is absolutely uninfluenced by any element of thought.

They, therefore, obey this urge with out any preliminaries and without any discrimination as to who they mate with. But with man and woman, the case is entirely different. They are sophisticated; the urge they feel is bound up with many associations; sexual union to them is not merely the means to the procreation of offspring nor is it confined to a particular mating season but is indulged in for pleasure and at all times. Further the factors of mutual satisfaction and a comparative permanence of relationship are absent in animals. These factors, which contribute to the fullness of pleasure in coitus among human beings, can be achieved only as a result of following a certain procedure which can be learnt by a study of the authoritative works on the Sexual Science.

There are others who say that one need not heed the commandments of religion, for their rewards are not of this world and who are at the same time doubtful whether they will bear any served fruit at all. Who but a fool would, there fore, allow the keeping in the hands of others of what is his own property? A humble pigeon in hand today is much better than a peacock promised for tomorrow. A copper coin in hand is better than a problematic gold coin. On these grounds some persons would discourage the observance of prescribed religious duties such as sacrifices, charities and acts of self-restraint. But, remarks Vatsyayana, the Shastras are not to be doubted, for they are of divine origin. The sacrificial rites observed for destruction of enemies or for pacification of the gods or for improvement of one's condition produce definite results if they are properly conducted.

The stars, the sun, the moon, the planets and the different signs of the celestial zodiac are, as it were, sentient indicators of good and evil. The existence of the individual in society involves obedience to the law of Varnashrama, i.e., the codified regulations for social divisions and their respective duties. And even when one has seed in hand, one does sow it on the ground in order to get more crops in future. For these reasons, one should obey the commandments of religion."

there are others who say that it is not necessary to acquire wealth For, sometimes it so happens that one's best efforts do not bring prosperity, while at other times, one is simply flooded with wealth with out having to move a finger. Well, says Vatsyayana, 10 is Destiny (Kala) which does everything. It is the arbiter of man's wealth or poverty, victory or defeat, and joy or sorrow. It made Vali the King of Heaven, it deposed him again from that exalted throne and it may again put him back there. But whether it is due to the action of Destiny or to other reasons, all enterprise for the pursuit of wealth evidently rests on one's will to acquire. Even things that are ordained to happen must await one's activity. The man who does nothing will enjoy no happiness, says Vatsyayana.

There are others who would forbid the enjoyment of sensual pleasures on the grounds that such enjoyment is prejudicial to the cultivation of wealth and religion which are both superior to it, and that it leads to association with the wicked, inclination to sins and crimes, uncleanliness and ultimately, misery. They contend that it also causes an inability to discriminate between right and wrong, unreliability, dishonour and meanness. They refer to the reports that many who had given themselves up to the pursuit of sensual pleasures have been ruined, not alone but with their followers. For instance, King Dandaka of the Bhoja dynasty had perished with all his kinsmen, friends and domains for having forcibly possessed a Brahmin girl. Indra, King of the gods, met with disaster for seducing Ahalya, the powerful Kichaka for wanting Draupadi, and Ravana for abducting Seeta. Many others have come to a violent end on account of their lust-argue the professors of moral conduct. Vatsyayana refutes this argument by pointing out that sexual satisfaction, equally like food, is essential to the maintenance of bodily health and consequently as wealth and religion.

Though evil effects low as a result of indulgence, passion has to be appeased; one cannot refrain from cooking food because beggars are about or from Sowing barley seeds because deer, come and eat up all the corn. Thus the sexual impulse is as necessary as the pursuit of religion or wealth.

In conclusion, it is said: "Man will attain perfect happiness by serving artha, kama and dharma in this manner. Cultured men engage in activities that do not endanger one's prospects in the other world, that do not entail loss of wealth and that are withal pleasant. They should do what favours the three objectives or two or even one of them but should never do what serves one of the objectives but militates against the other two."

CHAPTER 3
THE ARTS AND SCIENCES TO BE STUDIED

A MAN should receive instructions in the principles of Love and the accessory sciences at the same time as, and with out interfering with, his studies in the spiritual, moral and material sciences and the associated subjects. As for a woman, she should receive instructions in this science through preceptors before she has attained maturity; if she is married, she may do so with the approval of her husband. Some savants object to the education of women in the science and art of sex on the ground that women are not entitled to the study of the Shastras. But since there is no bar to women putting the principles of the Sexual Science to correct practical application and since such application is possible only after a working knowledge of the science, it is necessary that women also should learn it. This is true not only of this branch of knowledge, but also of other branches. Few have mastered the Shastras but everyone knows more or less about the practical application of the

Instructions given therein. The Science of Grammar has nothing to do w sacrificial sites, yet those who perform them have observe the rules of Grammar in uttering the want Persons ignorant of Astrology undertake work on auspicious days because the science is there; keepers of horses and elephants tame those animals without knowing the theories thereof; and subjects residing on the outlying fringes of an empire obey the king's law on the mere understanding that there is a king somewhere. There are many courtesans, princesses and daughters of ministers, military chiefs and bankers who are well read in the Science of Love Women should, therefore, learn the principles and technique of Love, either in whole or part, from a confidential friend and in secret.

There are sixty-four different arts to be learnt in order to be an adept in the science, young maids should practise them in strict privacy. Their instructors may be (I) the daughter of one's wet-nurse who has grown up along with one, (2) an intimate woman friend who can be trusted in every matter, (3) a mother's sister of the same age, (4) an old maid-servant enjoying the liberties of a mother's sister, (5) a mendicant woman who may be in one's confidence and (6) an elder sister with whom confidences may be exchanged regarding love affairs.

The sixty-four arts which should fit a girl to be a complete practitioner of the Art of Love are:

(1) Vocal music,

(2) instrumental music,

(3) dancing,

(4) painting in colours,

(5) decoration of the forehead,

(6) floor decoration with coloured powders,

(7) making of beds with flowers,

(8) colouring the teeth, garments, hair, nails and the body (i.e., staining, dyeing, colouring and painting the same),

(9) floor decoration with coloured stones and gems,

(10) making of different kinds of beds for different seasons and for different purposes,

(II) swimming and aquatic sports (Jala-krida),

(12) bewitching and spells to subdue and win others,

(13) stringing flowers into garlands and other ornaments for decorating the body,

(14) arranging flowers in the form of floral Crowns and chaplets,

(15) art of dressing for different occasions (private theatricals, masques, pageants, etc.).

(16) preparation of ear-rings with it shell and other materials,

(17) making of scents and other perfumery articles,

(18) matching of jewellery and denovating old ornaments,
(19) creating illusions (by magical tricks for the amusement and entertainment of guests),

(20) make-up, toilet and uses of beautifying agents,

(21) sleight of hand,

(22) art of cooking,

(23) preparation of different beverages, sweet and acid drinks, spiced alcoholic drinks and chutneys,

(24) sewing, darning and needlework of various kinds,

(25) making birds, flowers, etc., out of yarn or thread,

(26) mimicry of the sounds of the veena (a highly developed Indian guitar) and damruka (tabor),

(27) setting of puzzles and solving riddles,

(28) repartee in ex tempore verse (that is. when one person recites a verse, another individual follows with a recitation starting with the last quarter of the previous verse),

(29) participation in reciting verses difficult to interpret and not easy to pronounce,

(30) melodious and attuned reading (from the Ramayana and the Mahabharata, the epics of India),

(31) dramatic criticism and analysis of narratives,

(32) ex tempore filling up of the missing line of a verse,

(33) making different articles of furniture etc. from canes and reeds,

(34) wood engraving,

(35) carpentry,

(36) building-engineering,

(37) assaying of golden articles and gems,

(38) metallurgy,

(39) tinting or dyeing crystals and precious stones (mineralogy).

(40) gardening and care of plants and rules of the agricultural science,

(41) training rams, cocks and other birds for mock fights,
(42) teaching parrots and other birds to talk and sending messages through them,

(43) skill and dexterity in rubbing and massaging the body and the head, shampooing and dressing the hair,

(44) finger signals to convey messages,

(45) use of codes and cipher messages,

(46) knowledge of different vernaculars and dialects,

(47) floral decorations on carts, palanquins, horses, elephants etc.,

(48) knowledge of omens and augury,

(49) knowledge of apparatus and machinery,

(50) memory training or mental organs of subjects learned,
(51) recapitulation and lessons memory along with another,
(52) composing verse to order,

(53) knowledge of dictionaries and cyclopedias,

54) knowledge of poetics,

(55) rhetoric Or figures of speech,

(56) art of disguise.

(57) art of wearing clothes in the most appropriate way so that the pudenda are adequately covered in spite of violent movement,

(58) games of chance,

(50) games of dice, chess etc.,

(60) playing with balls and dolls for children,

(61) taming of pets, etiquette and good manners,

(62) knowledge of military strategy that helps a person to achieve victory over his opponent,

(63) physical culture and athletics, and

(64) art of knowing the character of a man from his features

A public woman versed in these sixty-four arts is called a ganika (courtesan) and is esteemed by the public, She is even honoured by kings and praised by leaders of fashion. She attracts them and is visited by them. Princesses and daughters of the nobility, versed in these arts, can hold the affections of their husbands even though the latter should have a thousand wives and mistresses. Even if an expert in these arts should lose her husband, she may make a comfortable living in strange places by virtue of these arts. A man well-versed in these arts, if he has a good tongue and a nice and charming manner with the ladies, can without much delay gain the favour of unknown women. Fortune smiles on men and women on the study of these arts, the application of which should depend upon considerations of time and locality.

CHAPTER 4
THE LIFE OF A CITIZEN

AFTER having finished his education, the accomplished man should set himself to the acquisition of wealth by acceptance of gifts (as in the case of a Brahmin), victory in war (as in the case of a Kshatriya), commerce (as in the case of a Vaishya) or service (as in the case of a Sudra); and having earned it by his efforts or come into it by succession or by both, should lead the life of an urban citizen. He should reside where he has a good chance of earning riches but should for preference select a city, a metropolis or a big or a small town for residence. He should build for himself a house with compartments for different uses near a source of water supply and with a garden and a summer house. The main building should have two portions—the outer and the inner ones. inner portion will be for the women and the domestic Offices, while the outer portion will consist of the drawing room. This outer room should contain a bed, richly mattressed, and somewhat depressed in the middle. should have pillows at the head and the bottom and should be covered with a perfectly white clean sheet. Near this bed there should be a small couch on which the sexual act should be performed so as not to soil the bed. Over the head of the bed there should be fixed on the wall a lotus-shaped bracket on which a coloured portrait or an image of one's favourite deity should be placed. Beneath this bracket should be placed a small table, one cubit in breadth, set against the wall. On this table the following articles, required for the night's enjoyments, should be arranged: balms and perfumed unguents, garlands, coloured waxen vessels, pots for holding perfumes, pomegranate rinds and prepared betels. There should be a spittoon on the floor near the bed; a lute (veena), a drawing slab, a pot with colours and brushes, a few books and wreaths of flowers, too, hung from elephants' tusks let into the wall. Near the bed upon the floor should be placed a circular chair with a back for resting the head on. Boards for the games of dice and chess should be placed against the wall. In a gallery outside the room cages for pet birds should be hung from ivory tusks fixed into the wall. In a private place outside should be kept instruments for shaping articles from timber, for sawing wood and for other kinds of games. In the summer house there should be, in the shade of trees, a swing draped with the most excellent cloth and a platform strewn over with flowers dropping from overhanging bowers of plants (so that women of the house or visiting mistresses can enjoy the beauty of the garden). Such should be the disposition of one's residence.

The man about town should, on rising before sun rise, ease himself, cleanse his teeth with brushes fashioned out of twigs and water, should moderately perfume himself with the help of pastes, aromatic fumes and scented extracts, should tint his lips with a little wax and lac dye, should look at himself in the mirror and should take into his hand his box of prepared betels and spices that sweeten the breath. All these done, he should set forth for the day's business. He should bathe every day, get his limbs massaged with oil every alternate day, use soap every third day, shave his face every fourth day and his private parts (pubic hairs) every fifth day, and use depilatories every tenth day. He should always stay in a covered place to check perspiration (i.e., should avoid going out into the open sun which causes perspiration and unpleasant body odour). He should take his meals in the morning and in the afternoon or evening.

After the morning meal he should train his talking or fighting birds, play indoor games with his friends and have a midday siesta. On rising from it, he should comb his hair and, having dressed well, should meet his friends either at a courtesan's place or at a gaming house or at a friend's in the company of a courtesan in order to discuss literature, drink wines, promenade in public gardens or have water sports. He should have songs and music in the evening. Then, after the drawing room has been decorated and well perfumed, he should sit on his bedstead with friends and await the arrival of his mistress. And if she should be late in coming, he should either send a woman messenger for her or go himself. When she is come, he and his friends should entertain her with loving and agreeable conversation and should please her by paying her small attentions and gifts. Should the mistress have come out to the man of fashion on a foul evening resulting in her clothes being disarranged or dusty, he should undertake to set her clothes and toilet right with his own hands without the help of his friends. Thus end the duties of the day.

The following are the social duties of a man about town, which he should observe as a matter of course:

1. ASSEMBLY OF CITIZENS ON FESTIVAL DAYS SACRED TO DEITIES (Ghatontvandhana): On these days the citizens should assemble at the Sarasvat Bhavan or the town institute hall where local or foreign artists (mainly singers) will display their skill. On the following day these artists will receive their due honour and rewards, when some of them may be retained and requested to give a further exhibition, while others may be dismissed according as their performance is liked or disliked by the beaux. Such assemblies should take place once in a fortnight or a month on a date previously arranged. The citizens must co-operate with one another and act in concert both in times of festivals as well as in the conduct of pastimes. The duty of a citizen to the community consists in assisting the members of the community on these occasions of general assembly and on occasions of sorrow by helping in the reception of the guests and artists and by offering consolation in times of sorrow.

2. SOCIAL GATHERINGS (Gosthisamavaya): Meetings at houses of courtesans, in dice-rooms (casinos) or at the Social gather- residence of friends or acquaintances who are equally matched in learning, intelligence, character, wealth and age are called Gosthis (clubs or salons). At these soirees there shall be agreeable discourse or questions of poetry

and the testing of knowledge of one another in the various arts. Glamorous and fascinating courtesans should be warmly received and duly honoured with attentions rendered by female servitors.

3. DRINKING PARTIES (Somapanaka): They should visit one another's house in rotation and there hold drinking parties. The drinks will consist of sweet wines (Madhu), Maireya (a kind of wine made in the town of Mira), spirits and fermented liquors (Asava) to the accompaniment of various kinds of salts, fruits, green salads and bitter, pungent and sour condiments and sauces that go well with the drinks. The courtesans should be given drink first and the gentle men will drink after them.

4. GARDEN PARTIES (Udyanagamana): Journeys to fashionable gardens should be made in the same manner as drinking parties, i.e. gardens of friends in the same social set should be selected for holding parties by rotation. Gentlemen should go there on horseback, well dressed and accompanied by courtesans and followed by servants, in the forenoon. There they should enjoy the day in various agreeable diversions and should engage themselves, to pass the time, in witnessing such pleasant pastimes as cock-fights, quail fights, ram-fights, games of chess and dice, dancing, acrobatics and theatricals etc. They should also in the summer season join in water sports in artificial tanks in which there are no noxious creatures like crocodiles etc. In the evening they should return from the garden after having received bouquets and garlands made of flowers from the garden.

{The first four categories of social enjoyment were not open to all classes of citizens but were confined to the wealthier classes. They condescended to join the ordinary citizens in the popular and community festivities}

5. POPULAR FESTIVITIES (Samasyakrida)': Gentle men should also take part in popular and community festivities, some of which are held in all States and some, again, are of local observance. They are participated in by all classes of people but gentlemen are required to show greater skill and proficiency in them than the ordinary people. Most prominent among these sports are those on the Diwali night

the full moon night preceding it (Kojagay Purnima, on which everyone should keep awake and make merry), and the thirteenth day of the first full-moon in spring (Madanatrayodashi).

Where a gentleman cannot procure company or would not mix with the available gentry, he should keep a suite of followers according to his means in order to keep up the traditional state of a gentleman.

Where a gentleman is the master of an establishment, his mistress will be either his wife or a courtesan; but where the principal party is a woman (either a wife, a widow or a courtesan), the order will be reversed, ie. the woman will act as if she were a gentleman and the object of her attentions will be a gentleman. The attendants in that case will, accordingly, differ in sex, a gentleman's retinue consisting of males and a woman's retinue, of females. The foregoing describes their social and individual duties.

The attendants of a fashionable gentleman will consist, firstly, of the Pithamarda (itinerant tutor of fashion and a sort of professor of all the arts), who is without any wealth or possessions and having no wives and children to look after (i.e. being alone in the world), has only him self to care for. The only furniture in his possession is a stool (shaped like the letter T, called Mallika); and as he is by no means indifferent to cleanliness, he carries with him some shampooing material and cosmetics. Such a man is a traveller from a country reputed for its culture of arts and is himself an expert in the sixty-four arts (see Ch. 111) and the Science of Sex. He earns his livelihood by giving instructions on the arts at social gatherings (gosthis) and by teaching prostitutes the rules of professional conduct.

The second class of men in a gentleman's retinue is the Bita (professional companion). He is one who possesses the qualifications for leading the life of a man of fashion, yet has squandered away all his fortune in quest of pleasure and has consequently lost his claim for being considered a beau.

He has a family to maintain. He is capable, by reason of his previous experience as a man of fashion, of giving authoritative opinion on many matters at social gatherings and assemblies in courtesans' residences and, in fact, maintains his livelihood by attaching himself to courtesans and gentlemen.'

"A Bita, in short, is a prostitute's procurer and pimp"

The third consists of the Vidushaka, the buffoon or jester. He has a deep knowledge of a particular section of music, is a good player, and enjoys the confidence of both gentlemen and their mistresses. He is either born poor or has squandered everything he had.

All these persons are employed as advisers in amorous liaison by both gentlemen and prostitutes. Mendicant women, female barbers, adulterous and barren wives (who have, because of it, been forsaken) and superannuated prostitutes are also employed as such.

Country people should encourage intelligent and inquisitive co-villagers to discuss the splendid mode of living of townsfolk and should follow it in a respectful frame of mind. They should also institute social gatherings in clubs etc., and should please the people by spending money. They should oblige fellow-villagers by helping the latter at every turn and by trying to oblige others as far as possible with their assistance in various matters.

At a social gathering (gosthi), a man of fashion should not speak too much in the Sanskrit language, nor should he speak too much in the vernacular. Judicious use of both dialects will bring him reputation. The wise will not join those gatherings that are not approved of by the élite, are convoked in a partisan spirit and are devoted to fault-finding and scandal-mongering. By participating in gatherings that conform to the wishes of the people, are meant for public entertainment and are devoted to pleasant pursuits, a learned man can succeed in being the beloved of men and women alike.

CHAPTER 5
THE DIFFERENT TYPES OF WOMEN FOR SEXUAL PLEASURES

SEXUAL union with a woman who never belonged, or was betrothed, to another and who is of the same caste group and (Varna) as the man of fashion and has been married to him according to the rules of the Holy Writ (that is, lawfully married) makes for offspring and glory and is customary. Sexual connection with a woman of a higher or lower caste or with a woman of the same caste who has been married to another man is prohibited and subject to penalties. Such connection with prostitutes or widows is neither prohibited nor recommended, it being exclusively for pleasure and not for offspring.

Thus there are three classes of women that are open to sexual enjoyment:

 (1) a wife or a maid of the same caste;

(2) a concubine that has been a widow; and

(3) a prostitute.

These three, then, are the permitted classes generally available for sexual relations. But Gonikaputra mentions a fourth class for sexual enjoyment who may be utilised only for special reasons and under special circumstances

(such as money, self-preservation from enemies or acquisition of friends).

This is the mistress who is the wife of another man. In ordinary circumstances it is a sin to approach another's wife. If, however, such a woman has been known to have had affairs with several other men, she may be enjoyed with the same impunity as a prostitute; even if she belongs to a higher caste there will be no offence against the commandments of religion. If, again, she is considered to be a widow who was widowed at a. mature age and has since remarried, though not of loose character, she may be enjoyed with impunity.

The special circumstances under which Gonikaputra allows adulterous sexual relations are as follows:

I. When a woman controls her husband who, a man of influence and wealth, has joined the enemies of the subject intending adultery. He thinks, if she grows intimate with him, she, out of love, will persuade her husband to abandon the enemy's party and join that of the subject.

2. When her husband is engaged in, and capable of, harming the subject and his wife is in a position to bring him round to the point of neutrality.

3. When her husband, persuaded through the wife's efforts to be friendly to the subject, is likely to assist him in opposing his enemies or in performing difficult tasks for him.

4. When it is likely that by allying himself with her, he can kill her husband and regain the fortune that had been the subject's own."

The case imagined is that in which a wicked man has by force or by unfair means deprived one of one's fortune and the aggrieved man enters into adulterous relations with the wicked man's wife in order to gain an opportunity of killing him and regaining his fortune.

5. When such clandestine relations are safe and a sure method of earning money. This applies to a subject who is poor and without any means of livelihood and who thinks that by making love to another's wife he may earn great wealth without exertion.

6. When there is the danger that a woman, yearning very passionately for the subject and finding him in different to her amorous advances, may denounce him and put him on his trial.

7. When she may spread false rumours or may bring against the subject some accusation of a nature that is easily believed by others, and which may not only injure his prestige but may even cause his death.

8. When the woman's husband has violated the chastity of the wife of the subject who wants, therefore to be revenged upon the malefactor by seducing his wife in return.

9. When she is likely to persuade her powerful and influential husband, whom she controls, to forsake the subject's side and join her adversaries out of spite for un requited love for the subject.

10. When the subject is commanded by his king to destroy an enemy of the latter who has gained admission into the harem of the king, the subject may make love to one of the king's mistresses to find out the concealed enemy.

11. When the woman whom the subject loves is under the power of another woman, the subject may make love to the latter in order to gain his beloved.

12. When a woman, out of love for the subject, is likely to help him get an unapproachable bride or a wealthy widow.

13. When it is found that her husband has allied himself with the subject's enemy, he may make love to the woman with the object of being able to put poison in that enemy's food at a suitable opportunity.

For these and similar other special reasons physical intimacy with the wives of other people may be under taken. However, it must be distinctly understood that it is permitted only for these purposes and not for the mere satisfaction of lust.

For these reasons, according to Charayana, a minister's or governor's wife, a king's wife, a woman of a royal family or any widow serving in the king's household may constitute a fifth class of mistresses. According to Suvarnanabha. a woman who leads the life of an ascetic (a nun) and is in the position of a widow (i.e., without a husband) may form sixth class of mistresses.

Ghotakamukha is of the opinion that a courtesan's daughter or a maid-servant who has not been previously deflowered may form a seventh class of mistresses.

Gonardiya would add still another class, the eighth. According to him, one's own wife, if she has reached full youth without having any sex experience, forms a special class of mistress, as a technique different from the one applicable to young wives is required in her case.

Vatsyayana, however, considers that all those extra classes are properly to be regarded as sub-classes of the four great classes mentioned earlier. But there are others who maintain that while Vatsyayana's classification of mistresses is correct, so far as women are concerned, the hermaphrodites who are resorted to for a special purpose make up a fifth class of mistresses.

There is only one class of males—the man of fashion --for operating in public. While a virgin retains her status so long as she has not slept with a man and loses that status when she has slept with one, a man may, without losing his status of a gentleman, marry a virgin or a widow or may patronise a courtesan.

The other class of lovers among men is the clandestine lover, whose counterpart is the fourth class among women (see above). A gentleman can be classified as a superior, moderate or inferior one according to the excellence, moderation or inferiority of his qualities. The qualities that make for excellence in man and woman will be described later in the chapter relating to prostitutes.

Vatsyayana absolutely forbids sexual contact with

(1) lepers, (2) lunatics, (3) outcasts, (4) those who cannot keep secrets, (5) those who solicit sexual satisfaction in public, (6) those who are no longer young, (7) albinos,

(8) extremely black women, (9) those having a bad body odour, (10) matrimonial relations of brothers sons, sisters or near relations, (11) wife's friends, (12) a female sanyasin (a nun). (13) wives of disciples, preceptors and relatives, etc., (14) friend's wives, (15) wives of Brahmins learned in the Vedas and (16) wives of kings.

Followers of Vabhravya are of the opinion that no woman who has had affairs with five men beside her husband need be spared. But Gonikaputra is of the opinion that even in such cases the wives of near relations, friends, learned Brahmins and kings must be excluded.

Intermediaries are necessary to approach the woman desired.

The following is a description of persons qualified as such:

Natural friends such as (a) play-mates of boyhood, (b) these bound by ties of mutual benefits or obligation, (c) those having similar pursuits and similar bents for pleasure, (d) class-mates, (e) intimate acquaintances who know each other's secrets and faults, f) acquaintances whose secrets one knows, (g) child of one's nurse, and (h) those who are honoured together.

Very valuable, indeed, are those friends with whose families cordially has existed for generations, whose words and actions are all open to each other and are never kept secret, who never act in a contrary manner and are obliging, constant in their affection, incorruptible and cannot be persuaded by others than one's friends and who never divulge their friends' plans.

According to Charayana, temporary friendship may be formed with (a) washermen, (b) barbers, (c) florists, (d) perfumers (e) publicans, (f) mendicants, (g) cowherds, (h) betel-and-chewing materials sellers, (i) goldsmiths, (j) pithamardas, (k) bitas, and (l) professional jesters or Vidushakas. Gentlemen of quality should also be friends with the wives of these people.

A friend who is also a friend of the desired woman and has served both with generous loyalty, particularly one, who is held in very great confidence by the woman concerned is the best person to act as an intermediary in love.

A qualified intermediary should have the following qualifications:

Such a person should be a good speaker, should not be afraid even when arraigned, should not feel ashamed even when reprimanded and should not feel diffident on any occasion. That person should be able to adjust or her conduct by a careful study of the facial expressions and movements of the eyes of the party approached should be able to discover the right opportunity to simulation, should possess the power to decide quickly when in doubt and, lastly, should be able to act quickly on his or her decisions.

Concluding, Vatsyayana observes: "A clever man who has helpers and is well up in the duties of a citizen and the significance of behaviour of men and women and exigencies of time and place, easily succeeds even in winning a woman beyond the reach of mortals.

CHAPTER 6
CONDUCT IN NEGOTIATING MARRIAGE

THE first requisites of a bride are that she should be of the same social class as the bridegroom and not have been betrothed to anybody else. She should come of a respectable family and have parents living. She should be at least three years younger than the bridegroom, well-behaved, rich and well-attended and possessed of a large number of relatives. She should be beautiful and accomplished and have auspicious marks on her body. She should not have excess or deficiency of teeth, nails, ears, hair and eyes, nor should she have undeveloped breasts, or be of a frail constitution.

Negotiations for marriage should be carried on through one's parents and relations and such other common relations and friends as have influence over the guardians of the bride. These friends will recite the apparent defects and astrological imperfections of other prospective bride grooms and the merits of birth, erudition and education of their own bridegroom, so that the bride's party becomes more eager than ever to give the bride away to him. Particularly should these friends represent the bridegroom's future prospects in such a light as appeals strongly to the tastes of the bride's mother. Such persons should be employed by the bridegroom's party as would predict accession by him of great wealth in future by citing the relative strength of the planets and the ascendant sign in his horoscope, the lines on his palm and the augury of birds.

Other persons also will approach the bride's | mother and tell her that this particular bridegroom was being pressed by such and such wealthy man to marry his daughter, until the mother becomes mad to marry her daughter to him.

One should select and marry a girl who pleases the mind and the eye. One who possesses auspicious marks, yet does not please the mind or the eye should not be given preference. If the girls under consideration have their respective defects, these should be carefully weighed; the one who pleases the mind and the eye should be favoured. Withal, the bride should be one whom the bridegroom's party will be proud to have and by marrying whom they will not incur the censure of their equals. Never depend merely on other men's recommendations or on your own caprice in giving away a girl in marriage. Both sides should be convinced, by consulting astrological signs, auguries, omens and other methods of ascertaining the future, that the union will turn out a happy one.

The following signs are to be noted when the bride groom's party views the bride for selection and if these are present, the bride should be rejected: If she is asleep at the time; if she is weeping; if she leaves the house in all these cases it may be presumed that her heart is not in the proposed marriage); if she has an unpronounceable or inauspicious name; if she hides herself; if she is betrothed to another previously, if she has a face like a horse or one with white spots (these denote very early widowhood); if she is mannish in build;' if she has low shoulders, badly shaped thighs or a protuberant forehead (these anomalies of growth and glandular dysfunction); if should have performed her father's cremation (this shows she has no near relations): if she should have had sexual experience before marriage (this is found out by looking for certain marks on her body); if she is already nubile; if she is dumb; if she is a friend or a cousin; if she is less than three years younger than the bridegroom; if she perspires in the hands or feet (such a girl is supposed to bring early death to her husband), and if she is named after the stars or rivers or trees or should have a name ending in 'L' or 'R'.

The guardians of the bride should, at the time of selection by the relations of the bridegroom, have her carefully and fashionably dressed and properly seated so that she may look beautiful.

At other times also she should be well made up every afternoon and encouraged to play with her girl friends. At public worships (yajna), weddings and festivities, where many people gather, she should be sent care fully and attractively dressed and shown to her best advantage, for a young girl is like an article for sale and should be displayed in like manner. Gentlemen arriving with a company of relatives and friends for the selection of the bride should be received with all courtesy, pleasant words and the customary presents (e.g., curds, whole betel leaves, etc.). The girl, well-dressed and ornamented, should be shown on some pretext or other. They should come to no decision regarding the giving away of the girl until she has been examined and the usual astrological consultations concluded.

The bridegroom's party coming to inspect the bride will be requested to have their bath and meals at the bride's place, but they should not accept the invitation and should put it off by saying that all will come in good time.

The wedding should take place according to the rules of Brahma, Prajapatya, Arsha or Daiva form as sanctioned by local custom.

In the matter of marriage and relationship by marriage it has been said: "Solution of puzzles and arguments playing games together, marriage and sexual intercourse should be practised among persons of equal position.

Practice of these with persons of a superior or an inferior position should be avoided. Where the bridegroom made to live like a servitor of the bride (i.e., when he marries above him) it is known as an ELEVATED (Uchcha) relationship; but intelligent men do not enter into such relationship.

Where, on the contrary, the bridegroom is so much respected by his matrimonial relations that he lords it over them it is a low (neecha) relationship; good people also condemn this.

But where both the bride groom's and the bride's parties are in a position to compete in mutually agreeable pastimes without constraint, in which first the one party and then the other win alternately i.e., where they are within the same set, know each other well and are evenly matched both in respect of cleverness and money), a connection by marriage is desirable. It is permissible for one to make an elevated alliance and go on behaving with humility among one's own kinsmen, but one must never contract a low alliance, which is particularly condemned by all good men."

CHAPTER 7
THE ART OF WINNING THE CONFIDENCE OF THE WIFE

WHEN the man of fashion has thus taken unto himself a suitable wife, his task will be to develop in the inexperienced wife a confidence in, and love for him so that she may derive pleasure from the act of sexual intercourse.

For the first three days after the wedding the husband and the wife should practise the strictest physical and mental continence (Brahmacharyya), eat food without sugar, salt or seasoning, and should sleep on the floor. For the next seven days they should have ceremonial ablutions, toilet and meals in each other's company-all to the accompaniment of song and music, should visit theatres and should pay attentions to their relations as well as to those who may have come to witness their marriage ceremony. This is recommended for people of all castes. Then, on the night of the tenth day, the husband should try to be intimate with her in strict privacy by beginning with soft words, so that she may not become nervous or concerned.

Referring to the first three days' stringent continence, which should even extend to silence between husband and wife, the followers of Vabhravya observe that this muteness and want of advances on the husband's part may cause the wife to think resent fully that she has been married to a dumb rustic lout and may even be disposed to rebuke him for his seeming lack of manly qualities.

Converse with her, replies Vatsyayana, gain her confidence by all means; but be sure to abstain at first from sexual pleasures. In approaching his wife the husband must not attempt to advance a single step by force. Women, being by nature delicate like flowers, require a tender approach. When they are forcibly approached by men (especially by those men with whom they are yet slightly acquainted) the memory of the violence will often make them unresponsive to sexual intercourse. A man should therefore, employ such technique as does not hurt the wife's sensibilities i.e., he should approach her according to her liking).

It is recognised that until husband has been able to gain the confidence of the wife the technique of love-play cannot be applied. In such a situation the husband should get into her confidence, embrace more and more. by adopting whatever course may be considered opportune in the circumstances such as, talking or playing with her favourite (female) companion. If, on the other hand, they are already acquainted with each other, the husband should begin wooing by embracing her in the manner she likes best.

This must be very brief, for a long embrace may surprise her. Let her be embraced in the upper portion or me body, for she can tolerate only such embrace. been wooed previously or is in the maturity of youth (i.e. if she is grown up), she may be embraced in a lighted room; but if she is a girl-wife or has not already been wooed, she should be embraced in the darkness, which will make her less shy.

After she has accepted the embrace, the husband should take a screw of prepared betel-leaf between his lips and put it to her mouth. If she would not accept it out of shyness, he should induce her, first with loving and conciliatory words, then with en treaties and extravagant oaths to the effect that he would kill himself if she did not accept it, then by beseeching her to give him a betel with her own lips and finally, by falling at her feet. Whether for overcoming the shyness of a female or for removing bar annoyance, no method is more efficacious than this, for no woman can refuse a lover kneeling at her feet. This is not only applicable to virgin-wives, but to all kinds of women. In the act of giving her the betel the husband should kiss her lips distinctly, softly and gracefully without making any sound.

When she has been gained over in this respect, he should encourage her to talk by asking her question about things she has seen or heard about pretending his own ignorance about them, and which can be answered in a few words. If she remains silent, she should not be hustled but plied affectionately with the same questions again and again. If the bride does not answer still, he should press the questions, for, as Ghotakamukha remarks, all brides tolerate the wooing's of their husbands but do not themselves utter so much as a single word, even if sexually roused, because of their natural and instinctive shyness. If questions are persisted in, she will reply by nodding and shaking her head; but if she is annoyed or angry with the man, she may not even do that. She should be asked questions like these: "Do you want me?" "Do you like me "Can you love me?" She may not reply at first but when she is hard pressed, she will give a favourable reply by nodding her head affirmatively.

If she discovers, however, that the husband is trying to trap her into a conversation, she may give him entirely misleading replies.

When the wife has been wooed by the husband be forehand, conversation may be carried on through the intermediacy of a female friend of hers who is in the confidence of both. On such an occasion when the friend replies for the girl, the latter will smile coyly with her head bent down. If the friend, out of fun, gives an exaggerated account of her liking for the young man, the wife will scold her and quarrel with her. And the friend should invent further stories, adding, "She says so," making the wife discard her reserve more and more. The husband should now ask the bride directly if these stories are true.

The bride will naturally remain silent but on being pressed hard, she will say prettily, "I won't tell " in such a low whisper that she may hardly be heard. At this stage she will every now and then throw covert glances at the husband and smile archly. The barriers of reserve drawn, the pair will now talk with growing ease and the friend should discreetly withdraw.

When conversation has become unreserved, the bride will place before the husband, without speaking, the betel, unguents and garlands he had asked for earlier, or she will tie them up in a corner of his wrapper. This will be a signal for the husband to take advantage of her nearness by pressing the nipples of her young breasts gently with the ends of his fingers in the **achhuritaka** fashion. If she forbids or prevents him from doing this, he should offer not to do it again if she would embrace him, and in this manner cause her to embrace him. While thus engaged, he should pass his hand repeatedly over her body as far as the navel. Now that her breasts have been pressed by his body during the embrace, the husband should take her on his lap by and by, gently rub her body and tickle her mammae and kiss and press with his teeth her lips and try more and more to gain her acquiescence.

If she will not yield to him, he should even half seriously threaten her with words like these: I will make marks with my teeth on your lips and with my nails on your breasts, and then I will make similar marks on my own body. I will tell your female friends that you have done so to me. How will you then explain it to them? With such words and other ways, as create fear and confidence in the minds of very young persons, should the husband gain her over to his wishes.

This is how far the husband should proceed on the first night of intimacy. On the second and third nights, when the bride has gained more confidence, the husband should feel the whole of her body with his hands, extending them to the region of her breasts, thighs and the genitalia.

This is how it should be brought about: The man should begin by kissing her whole body above the waist, place his hand on her thigh and press it gently. If he succeeds, he should work his way up and gently massage the upper part of it (i.e., the joints of her thighs). If she protests, or prevents him from doing this, he should tell her repeatedly that there is no harm in it and persuade her to let him do it. He should also make her breath less by kissing her and caressing or titillating her mammillie. When she has come to find pleasure in the massaging of her thighs, he should fondle her genitalia and on the pretext of rubbing her body, loosen her girdle, take off her lower and intimate garments and disrobe her with his own hands. Then he should begin again the caressing of the upper joints of her thighs. Thus far on the second and the third nights. The first initiation to coitus must not take place before she has had her first menstrual period after marriage. Particular care should be taken that there is no actual union of the organs before she is physically and psychologically prepared for it. If she is not yet ready for the act, the man should not hustle her into sufferance of a premature practice. Rather, he should teach her the sixty-four arts and help her into maturity by showing his love for her by signs and gestures and by using the accessory processes described above. He should also promise to be faithful to her in future and dispel all her fears of co-wives or rival women. And only when she has developed into maturity and, incidentally, overcome her bashfulness, should he effect the actual coitus and that in such a manner as not to frighten her.

Why these preliminaries. Why wait and not satisfy one's passion at the first opportunity the husband finds the wife alone?

If the man is acting according to the inclinations of his wife and so gains her confidence, she, in return, will place her confidence in him and be the willing Slave of his love-desire.

If she be always too willing to yield to her master's desire, she will be so passive an agent as to be unresponsive; if she be too unwilling, any attempt at physical intimacy will be a failure. Therefore, a man should see to it that she co-operates in the sexual act of her own free will and with intense pleasure. She should stand neither in awe nor in fear of her husband. The person who knows the pleasant method of attracting a girl's love by gaining her confidence and intimacy and by increasing her own self-esteem at the same time is sure to be very dear to women. On the other hand, the man who neglects a girl because of her shyness is considered by her as a fool ignorant of the ways of a maid and as such despised like a brute. The man who, without caring to understand a girl's psychology, attempts to take or takes possession of her body by force, only succeeds in arousing the fear, horror, concern and hatred of the girl. Deprived of the affection and sympathetic understanding she longs for, she becomes obsessed with anxiety which makes her nervous, uneasy, and dejected. She either suddenly becomes a hater of the whole male sex altogether or, hating her own husband, gives herself to other men as a form of revenge.

CHAPTER 8
COURTSHIP OF YOUNG GIRLS FOR MARRIAGE

A NEEDY or destitute though well-connected and otherwise qualified man, a beautiful and cultured man without good connections, a rich man who is always quarrelling with his neighbours, a man who is dependent upon his parents and brothers, or a man who is admitted into others' houses on account of his child-like behaviour but is not regarded seriously—these cannot select their brides by negotiation because the brides' people will not have them. Since very few are so endowed as to be perfect, desirable husbands, one should be careful to gain the affection of a suitable girl from her very childhood, so that when she grows up she would overlook his shortcomings and choose him for husband. It is found that in the Deccan (Dakshinapalha) orphan boys growing up in neglect in the families of their maternal uncles succeed, by means of courtship, in marrying their cousins, normally unavailable to them by reason of their wealth, or even though they may be previously betrothed to others; also in making themselves desired by unrelated girls of marriageable age. Such ways of gaining over the love of a young girl with the object of lawfully marrying her is, according to Ghotakamukha, quite to be approved.

Courting of young girls may be done by two kinds of men: adolescents and those who have attained manhood.

The boy lover should spend his time with the girl he loves and amuse her with various games and diversions natural to their age and acquaintance, such as assisting her in picking and collecting flowers and making garlands out of them. He should play with her the games of a doll's house and doll children, also that of preparing and cooking food with dust and mud.

He should behave appropriately to the extent of his intimacy with the girl and to his and her age (i.e., a boy should behave like a boy or, if he is almost mature and the girl yet young, then also like a boy and so on).

He should also play, with her and her attendants and companions, those games that are locally popular and there fore well-known and agreeable to the latter, such as playing with dice, playing with cards, tricks with long strips of cloth, wagers regarding things held within the closed palm (i.e. games of odds and evens), catching a furiously wagging middle finger, juggling with six pebbles, etc. in addition to this he should also play such outdoor games played by several persons together that cause physical exertion, such as catching-the-thief (Sunimeelitaka, an indigenous form of black-fruit form of hide-and-seek), playing with seeds or game (Aravdhika), salt-caravan (Lavanabithika), bird's flight (anilatadika, in which the arms are stretched like the wings of a bird and the player runs in a circle), wheat dealing

(Godhumapunjika, in which a few small coins and handfuls of wheat are divided among the players and mock dealing is carried on), blind-man's buff, gymnastic exercises and other children's games prevalent in the locality in company with the girl, her friends and female attendants.

A grown-up young man should invariably keep on good terms with the woman who is in the intimate confidence of the girl to be courted and should also show great kindness to her. He should make sure that she (the confidante) is willing to act on his behalf. He should attach to himself the daughter of the girl's nurse by rendering her pleasant and valuable services. In this way she may not cause any obstruction to the young man's design when he has unfolded his plan to her and may effect a meeting between him and the desired girl or, even when she has not been directly asked to do so, may arrange a lovers' meeting. Further, though she may not have definitely known about his intention, she may on account of her liking for the young man cause the courted girl to feel attracted to him by reciting his qualities.

In this way he should do whatever he may find very delightful to the beloved girl and should get for her whatever she may desire to possess. He should procure and unstintedly present her with those rare playthings that he knows are possessed by very few other girls. Among the latter should be a great number of gaily decorated balls (or pins) of different sizes and shapes. These should be supplied to her at short intervals, so that she may select from these the ones she may like. Likewise, dolls made out of cloth, thread, wood, buffalo-horn, ivory, wax, flower, powdered rice and clay, also miniature cooking utensils should be sent to her for acceptance. Representations of figure wood, such as human couples in sexual embrace and of! gods and their abodes, should also be shown. Temples made of clay, bamboo or wood, dedicated to various goddesses; and rams or goats or sheep in pairs, and cages for parrots, pigeons, jays in couples, cuckoos, starlings, quails, cocks and partridges-made of mud, split bamboo or timber-should be specially prepared for her, and water bowls and vessels with elegant figures of various designs and colours engraved on them, various curious instruments, toy veenas (the Indian guitar), small palettes for toilet purposes, lacquer red, powdered colours such as collyrium for painting, sandalwood, kum-kum, betel, betel-nuts and whatever other thing may be appropriate to the time should be shown to her. Should the suitor be in a position to provide these, he should present these things at different times whenever he gets a good opportunity of meeting her. But some of these should be given in secret and some that can be given in public be offered to her publicly, according to circumstances. In short, he should try to perform meticulously those tasks that would make him well thought of by everybody (connected with the girl) as the fulfiller of their desires and that would make her look upon him as one who would get for her everything she desired. After that, he should get her to see him in some place privately, and at that meeting should speak to her confidentially. He should explain to her that the reason for his giving presents in secret was the fear of his own superiors and should also add that another girl had greatly desired and bad tried hard to have from him the presents he had made her, but without success. When her liking begins to show signs of increasing he should narrate to her those agreeable stories that she likes best to hear, if she expresses a wish to hear them. In this way she will become more and more fond of him. If he comes to know that she takes delight in such interesting things as tricks of magic, he should entertain her by performing various tricks of jugglery, or if she feels a great curiosity to see a performance of various arts, he should show his own skill in them. He should please her with tuneful music, if she is fond of music. On the full-moon night of Autumn (Kojagar) when everyone must keep awake and make merry, on the eighth day of the new moon in the month of Agrahayana (pre-winter) when people feast at night after fasting the whole day, on the moonlit night in the month of Kartik (autumn) when girls worship the starry heavens, on festival days and days devoted to the gods, on days when eclipses take place and on occasions when the beloved girl has visited one's household he should present her with bouquets of flowers, beautifully coloured chaplets for the head and ear-ornaments made of wax, rings and other ornaments. He should, of course, do these if he is sure that no exception will be taken to those presents.

The daughter of her nurse should persuade the girl that this particular young man is distinguished from all others and, in order to unite him to her, should get her to study the sixty-four arts. He should reveal his own experience and great skill in the arts to his beloved girl on the pretext of giving her instruction in these arts. He should always be dressed fashionably so that he may always appear immaculate.

The suitor should understand from signs and symptoms exhibited by the girl whether she has become attracted to him. For it often happens that young women wish always to see those intimately acquainted young men for whom they have conceived a strong liking; but they do not, out of shyness, make any effort themselves to manifest their desire.

The signs and actions by which a bashful maiden expresses her preference for a suitor are of two kinds: (i) physical and (ii) mental. Arch looks, blushes, etc.. constitute the physical signs and the use of equivocal words constitutes the mental sign. When a maiden has conceived a love for a young man, she never looks the man straight in the face and becomes abashed when she is looked at by him. But on some occasions she shows her beautiful limbs -breasts, upper arm, etc.-to him just for a moment under the pretext of adjusting her dress. And when the suitor is absent-minded or alone or when he has gone away from her side she looks long and covertly at him. When any question is asked by the suitor, she smiles just a little and with lowered eyes speaks almost unintelligible words slowly a in a low voice with indistinct and broken sentences. delights to be near him for a long time. When she is at a short distance she speaks to her relatives, friends and attendants with arched brows and flashing looks to all his attention. She does not wish to leave his presence, under some pretext or other. She laughs at whatever small things she observes and spins cut her talks for a long time in order to stay on near him. She embraces and kisses a child sitting on her lap and draws ornamental marks on the forehead of her female attendants, arranges the hair of her female relatives and performs other sportive and graceful movements so as to be near him. She confides in and trusts the friends of her suitor, gives importance to their words and acts accordingly. She engages in pleasant conversation with the suitor's attendants, also plays dice, etc. with them and even orders them to do her own behests as if she were already their mistress. When they recount to others stories about her suitor she pricks up her ears and listens attentively. She visits the suitor's home at the request of her nurse's daughter and with her, as intermediary, converses and plays dice with him. She avoids being seen by her lover when she is not dressed up, deco rated and ornamented. Should he beg for a souvenir in the shape of an ornament-an ear-ring, a ring or a garland of flowers-she takes it off very slowly and hands it over to her female attendant. She always wears all those ornaments that have been presented by the suitor. She becomes dejected when other suitors are talked about and refuses to have anything to do with the parties of other suitors or with any individual who may support any of them.

In conclusion, it is stated: "A man should look care fully for the outward signs and actions denoting love that have been described above in the courted girl and apply himself further to the task of winning her after a careful consideration of these. A juvenile maiden should be won with childlike sports, a youthful maiden with one's skill in the arts and a maiden of advanced age with the help of persons in whom she confides."

CHAPTER 9
HOW TO WIN A WIFE AND A HUSBAND

THE lover should press his suit in the appropriate manner when a girl has exhibited by outward signs and emotions her love for him, as described in the previous chapter. He should try to gain her entirely over by various ways and means.

For example, while playing with her at dice or any other game, he should pretend a quarrel with we and should intentionally take hold of her hand with amorous gestures so that she may regard herself as being virtually married to him. He should practise upon her the various kinds of embraces, such as the touching or Slight-contact embrace or any other varieties of preliminary embrace, according as opportunity offers itself. The girl should be shown representations of couples of human beings or geese, and such other things as symbolise his intention, executed by nail-marking on leaves of trees. This, however, should be done occasionally. When engaged in water sports, he should dive at a distance from her and, swimming under water, come up close to her and emerge at her side after touching her body. When the festival of the New Foliage (a spring-time festival) is on, he should make significant markings on new leaves from which she may understand his appeal. He should dilate on the misery and the pangs he suffers on her ac count without, however, really feeling miserable and should also relate, in course of other topics, beautiful dreams of having been united to her. He should manage to seat him self by the side of his beloved at dramatic performances or at social gatherings, where he should touch her on some pretext or other. To rest his body against hers he should press her foot with his. When he is successful in this he shot slowly press each of her toes with his own and should rub the nails of her toes with his big toe.

If he succeeds in this he should attempt to touch different other parts of her body, making for regions higher up. In so doing, he should proceed gradually in the manner described above so that she may get used to it.

If the sweetheart happens to be washing his feet, he should pinch her fingers between his toes. In giving or receiving anything to or from her he should mark it with his nails. If she gives him water to wash his mouth, he should release it in a spray. When alone with her in a lonely place or in the dark and also while sitting on the same part of the bed, he should get her gradually used to caresses and nail scratching's: there he should make a declaration of his desire through gestures and actions, without, however, speaking in a manner that may distress or embarrass her. He should say to her," I have something to tell you in private and should deduce her degree of response to his appeal from her behaviour, in the manner to be described later when dealing with the winning of others' wives.?

When the suitor is in this way sure that the sweetheart is willing to receive his advances, he should feign illness and thus bring her to his residence for news of him. When she comes there he should engage her in massaging his forehead and head by saying that he has had a headache, etc. He should intentionally take hold of her hand with significant gestures (pressure, touching with the lips etc.), and should place on his eyes and forehead. As for the medicine that would relieve his feigned illness, he should tell her that her ministrations are all the medicine necessary for his cure. When she wants to leave him he should bid her good-bye, repeatedly saying, "You must minister to me, for none but you can do it and with an earnest request to her to come and see him again. This device of illness should be continued for three days and three nights and when the sweetheart has arrived on each occasion, fine arts (like music etc.) should be practised and stories narrated for a considerable time by those present so that she, out of interest in the display of arts or in the stories, may stay with him for a long time. To create the girl's confidence (i.e., to show that his advances have nothing to cause worry or anxiety) he should mix with other women present there to al greater extent than before, but should take care not to express words of preferment to any, so that one of them may not be encouraged to engage in a love anal with him; for, says Ghotakamukha, however deep may be a maiden's love, there can be no success for a man if he does not talk long and earnestly to her. At last when the suitor is sure that his sweetheart, after long and varied approaches, has become eager to give herself up to him, he should attempt sexual intercourse with her. The appropriate time for this is evening, night and the dark when women become sexually impassioned and desire union. At these times they become less timid and do not reject the advances of their lovers, who should, therefore, take advantage of these periods for the gratification of their desire. This, in fact, is a common practice.

When it is found impossible for the suitor to carry on all the endeavours alone and by himself, the daughter of the nurse or a female friend of the sweetheart in whom she con fides and/or who has grasped the intentions of the suitor should be made to induce the girl on a different pretext to come, without divulging his design to her, to the suitor. Then he should proceed to apply the technique of love-play as described earlier. Or he should even before this send a trusted female servant of hers to live with the girl as her friend and should then gain her with the latter's help.

A maiden who has exhibited signs and symptoms of love for a suitor in a public place, such as an assembly of people for sacrificial rites, weddings, religious festivals, secular festivities (Cf. popular festivities and festival days sacred to deities, Ch. IV) or pastimes or public shows (theatres, dances etc.) and whose behaviour has been closely observed, will certainly agree to a sexual union if approach ed when she is alone in a secluded place. . If women of observed inclinations are approached in a suitable manner and at the proper time and in the proper place, says Vatsyayana, there cannot be any coldness on their part and they do not turn away from their lovers.

There are certain circumstances in which a maiden should exert herself to secure a husband. When, for example, she is possessed of good qualities such as beauty, wealth etc., and is well bred though born in a humble family; or when, being well-connected, she has no wealth or near relatives and is, therefore, not offered the hand of young men of an equal social status; or when, having lost her parents, she is brought up in her maternal uncle's family but is not being given in marriage, she should set herself the task of bringing about her own marriage on attaining maturity. Such a girl should make loving advances to a well-qualified, strong and handsome young man with whom she had been on affectionate terms in childhood or to one who, in her judgment, would have her without the consent or approval of his parents on account of his own uncontrollable passion for her. She should attach him to herself with the help of such technique as is pleasing and beneficial to him and by seeing and meeting him often and again. Her mother, along with her female friends and the daughter of her nurse, should help her in drawing him towards her by arranging frequent meetings. If her own mother is dead, the adoptive mother should do so.

Such a maiden should go alone and in secret with flowers, Perfumes and screws of betel (tambula) in her hand to the prospective husband's place late in the afternoon and present these to him. She should display her proficiency in artistic pursuits and massage or nursing of the head. She should also engage in such conversation as is agreeable to him. Altogether, she should behave in the same manner as a male suitor would behave in respect of a maiden. But even when she experiences the most powerful sexual excitement she should not make advances with the object of having sexual intercourse. The leading role must be left to the male. The preceptors maintain that although a young woman may love a man ever so much, she must not offer herself or make the first overtures, for a girl who does this loses her dignity and is liable to be scorned and rejected and will never be fortunate in winning the affection of the lover.

The advances of the prospective husband should not however, be rejected. On the contrary, they should be reciprocated with all the appearances of pleasure. When she is embraced she should not betray any concern or nervousness or any change of demeanour. If the lover should indulge in such manifestations of love as an attractive gesture or attractive method of caressing, she should acknowledge it with inarticulate sounds indicative of pleasure, as if she had never known of these joys before so that he may not think her as forward. When he attempts to kiss her mouth she should offer feeble resistance so as to compel him to use force to gain his end. When the lover importunes her to touch his pudenda with her fingers as a pointer of his intention she should do so with an appearance of very great reluctance and considerable embarrassment. She should not be very much unrestrained herself, though importuned in this manner, until she is sure that her man has conceived a true love and a great passion for her and, moreover, will not change his mind. Only then should she expedite the process by which they would step out of adolescence (i.e., sexual intercourse). When she has stepped out of virginity she should reveal it to her intimate friends etc., so that their marriage according to Gandharva rites' may be know to all.

Gandharva marriage, common among the early Aryans, called for no sacred rites or ceremonies but depended for its validity on mutual recognition by a couple of their married state. This form suffered a suppression in the post-Buddhist Hindu society

Concluding, Vatsyayana observes: "A maiden who is much sought after should marry one whom she finds attractive, dependable, agreeable, obedient to her, and also capable of giving her protection. Even where it is customary for a girl. without taking into consideration qualities like lineage, beauty, culture and bravery, to choose a husband having several wives merely for the sake of his wealth, she should not reject a suitor who has all these qualities except wealth, is obedient, capable and strong and presses his suit in the proper manner (i.e., by being agreeable etc.). For it is better to be the sole wife of a husband who is without qualities, wealth and good looks than to be one among several wives of a well-qualified, handsome and attractive husband. Again, wealthy men often have many wives and are slaves to their whims and desires. Although their wives have all the material sources of external enjoyment of life, they have little satisfaction in their hearts. A low-born man or a man of low mind or an old man or a man who is much given to travelling in foreign lands, though he may make the proper overtures for marriage, is not an ideal partner for union. A man who indulges in promiscuous sexual relationships to satisfy his own passion or one who is deceitful, addicted to boasting and gambling or already with many wives or children or with both, is never to be considered fit for union. If all the men who are pressing their suits are evenly qualified, one of them must be preferred; even in that case the suitor who possesses the qualities that are liked by her should be considered to be the best, for he will be the man of her love."

CHAPTER 10
FORMS OF MARRIAGE BETWEEN YOUNG LOVERS

IF frequent meetings with the sweetheart cannot be arranged the suitor should gain over the daughter of her nurse to his interest by agreeable and useful means and should send her to the girl.

This intermediary (the daughter of the nurse) should, in the course of conversation, without disclosing the fact of her being commissioned by the Suitor and in such a way as not to cause her to suspect that she has been engaged by him, draw the girl's mind to him by describing the qualities of the suitor, particularly enlarging upon those qualities that are pleasing to her. The daughter of the nurse should, moreover, dilate upon those disqualifications of rival suitors for which the girl has a distaste. She should show how the parents of the girl are unable to recognise true merit in the suitors and are moved by greed of wealth; also how her relations are fickle and inconsiderate. The nurse's daughter should also point out to her how other maidens of ancient times in the same predicament, such as Shakuntala and others who had secured husbands of their own choice, were happy ever afterwards through union with their lovers. She should further reason that though her parents might give her away into a great and noble family, it was frequently found that the girls who married in such families became wretched and miserable and were ultimately even abandoned by their husbands through the machinations of rival co-wives.

She should dwell at length on the unbroken happiness and good fortune of the monogamous couple and the continual love, constancy, obedience, and affection of the husband in that state. When the daughter of the nurse will understand that the maiden has conceived a love for the suitor she should remove. by reasoning with her, her apprehensions, fear, hesitation, suspicion and feeling of shame. a word, she should act the whole part of a female intermediary by telling the girl all about the suitor's affection for her, the places he frequented and the endeavours he made to meet her and by frequently repeating that she should behave in his presence as if she did not know any thing about the suitor and also that if he should take her (the girl) away forcibly, no blame would attach to her as she would be well married, after all.

If the maiden is agreeable to this, the suitor should take her to a secluded place and bring sacrificial fire from the house of a Brahmin practising Vedic rites. He should cause some kusha grass to be spread around the fire and, according to the family custom, should perform worship (Homa). After this, the bridegroom and the bride should walk round the fire three times. When this has been done, the parents of the bride should be informed. The considered opinion of the Shastras (scriptures) is that a marriage consecrated solemnly in the presence of the sacrificial fire cannot be set aside or annulled later. After the wedding the wife should be relieved of her virginity and the news of the marriage should be gradually broken to the bridegroom's kinsmen and relations. Measures should be so taken that the kinsfolk of the bride recognise the marriage and consign her to the bridegroom's care out of a desire to avoid a family scandal and fear of State punishment. When this is achieved, they should be reconciled by the gift of affectionate presents and by amiable behaviour.

In those cases where the parties are willing but a better formal marriage cannot be arranged, they should try to solemnise it in the Gandharva form.

If the girl does not agree to marry in this fashion (but at the same time entertains a feeling of preference for the suitor), the suitor should win over, by means of gifts, a respectable lady who is known to be on intimate terms with the girl and is also well acquainted with the suitor and one whom he can trust and should get her to induce the girl to come to a suitable place on another pretext. When this has been done, consecrated fire should be brought from a Brahmin practitioner of Vedic rites and the ceremony marriage gone through as described before.

Or, if the marriage of the sweetheart with a rival suitor draws near, a female neighbour of hers, enlisted in support of the lover, should describe the disqualifications of the chosen bridegroom to the mother of the bride so forcefully as to cause the mother to relent. Then, when the mother of the girl has consented to marry her daughter to the lover, he should be summoned to that neighbour's house at night, consecrated fire should be brought and the marriage performed as described already.

In the alternative, the suitor should contrive to become a great friend of the brother of the sweetheart who may be of the same age as himself and who may be addicted to a courtesan or mistress or may have an intrigue with the wife of another man. He should give the brother valuable assistance in such matters and occasional gifts of fancied things. This should go on for a long time. He should ultimately acquaint him with his intentions and confess his great love for his sister, for young men often go even to the extent of giving up their lives for the sake of those friends who are of the same age and have similar pastimes and pursuits. Therefore, the brother will have the girl brought to the lover on some pretext and, having brought fire from the house of a Brahmin, will give his sister away in marriage as described above.

Or, on the eighth night after full moon in Agrahayana (in late autumn; on this occasion women fasted the whole day and feasted in the evening) the daughter of the nurse, won over by the suitor, may give the maiden some strong wine or some other intoxicant and, on the pretext of moving about on her own business, may take the girl to a secure place assigned by the suitor. There the girl may be plied with more drinks and the like (this being a festival day) and when she has become stupefied with intoxication she may be relieved of her virginity, and later, when she has recovered from intoxication, married in the manner described before i.e., before the sacred fire). Or while the maiden is sleeping in a room alone but for the daughter of her nurse, the suitor may steal in and, having persuaded the latter not to disclose the occurrence, possess the girl in a sleeping state and marry her subsequently in the manner aforesaid.

Or the suitor may, on receipt of information that the maiden has gone to another village or to a garden in the neighbourhood, go there with a large number of armed men and, after having beaten or killed the guards of the girl, forcibly carry her off and proceed as before.

Dwelling on the relative merits of the several forms of marriage prevalent in the country, Vatsyayana observes : Each form is better than the one that follows it, on account of its being more in accordance with the commands of religion. Therefore, only when it is impossible to adopt the former into practice should the latter be resorted to.

" Though the Gandharva form of marriage has been assigned a middle position, yet it is very much esteemed and respected because it is born of love and the fruit of all good marriages is love. Gandharva marriages give happiness; they involve none of the troubles of match-making nor those of selection (as in marriages of convenience) and are resorted to out of abundance of love. It is, there fore, the best of all forms of marriage in the opinion of preceptors."

This has a few mythological precedents, such as the marriage of Krishna and Rukmini and of Arjuna and Subhadra. Nevertheless, it was considered a very low and sinful form of marriage in later times, especially where the girl was unwilling.

CHAPTER 11
CLASSIFICATION OF SEXUAL UNIONS

The act of sexual union is dependent upon (a) psychological and (6) physical factors.

The psychological factor consists of a background of sexual attraction between a man and a woman and immediate conditions, such as the desire to meet in coitus etc. With these are often associated particular accessory processes that contribute to the heightening of the desire and also to the physical preparation of both the partners in the act. From the physical standpoint the act consists in

(I)   the introduction and penetration of the phallus into the vaginal canal of the female,

(II)   The onset of rhythmic coital movements on the part of one or both and

(III)   Ejaculation of the seminal fluid on the part of the male and orgasm on the part of the female.

The practicability of the act of penetration and the pleasure to be derived from coitus, therefore, become ultimately a question of successful adjustment between the male and the female organs or, as Vatsyayana points out, to their size, duration of activity and character of action.

On the subject of size of the male and the female organs, Vatsyayana divides the male organ (lingam) into Classification ac- three classes, viz.,

(1) the Rabbit, (2) the Bull and (3) the Horse.

The Rabbit is the man with the shortest organ, being six digits in length. The Bull has the average medium length, being nine digits long. The Horse is the outsize class, being twelve digits long. In each class the circumference corresponds more or less to the length of the organ.

A digit is the breadth of one finger measured on the back of the hand, - approximately three-fourth of an inch.

Similarly the female organ is divided, according to the size of the vagina, into three classes, viz.,

(1) the Doe, (2) the Mare and (3) the She elephant.

The woman of the Doe class has the shortest vagina, being equal to six digits. The Mare class has a depth of nine digits and the She-elephant has the greatest depth, being twelve digits.

The circumference of the vaginal canal in all the three classes is in proportion to the depth of the organ. The vaginal circumference can, however, be stretched to a bigger size.

The union of a Rabbit male with a Doe female is called an equal fit on account of the perfect correspondence between the two organs. So also are union between a Bull and a Mare and that between a Horse and a She-elephant.

In case of disparity (mis-matching) in the respective dimensions of the organs of the two parties, there may be six forms of "unequal union," e.g.,

(1) Union between a Rabbit and a Mare.

(2) Union between a Rabbit and a She-elephant.

(3) Union between a Bull and a Doe.

(4) Union between a Bull and a She-elephant.

(5) Union between a Horse and a Doe.

(6) Union between a Horse and a Mare.

These, again, can be divided into two classes, the tight fit and the loose-fit. Where the male organ exceeds the female's in point of size, as in cases 3 and 6, the entire length of the membrum virile cannot be introduced without difficulty. Such a union is called a tight-fit.

In case 5, however, the introduction will be still more partial on account of the membrum virile being the largest and the genital passage being the narrowest, and coitus may be a painful affair. This is called the tighter fit. Where again, the female organ exceeds the phallus in point of size the union is called a loose-fit, as in cases I and 4. In such coitus introduction can be effected to the full length of the phallus without, however, reaching the extreme depth of the vagina. In case 4, however penial entry is full without reaching half the extent of the vaginal canal and coital friction is so light on account of the dissimilarity of dimensions of the two organs as to afford much less pleasure than would be normal. This is called the looser-fit.

Of all these kinds of union, the equal-fit is the best, the tight-fit and the loose-fit are fair and the tighter fit and the looser-fit are the worst. Between the tight-fit and the loose-fit the former is certainly the better, for it satisfies the female partner more than the latter. indeed, the tight-fit gives her greater voluptuous pleasure. For this reason, she spreads her thighs wide apart so as to facilitate the introduction of the tumescent membrum (phallus) which, on account of its ampler girth, causes harder friction against the vaginal wall and relieves in a greater degree the itching sensation felt by the woman than in the loose-fit in which the woman cannot obtain satisfactory penial friction even by putting one thigh upon the other in an attempt to narrow down the orifice as far as possible and cannot, therefore, obtain genuine relief of the itching.

It has been said, "Even if a man of small parts be passionate or long of action, he cannot endear himself to a woman on account of his inability to relieve the itching sensation in a woman."

A man is termed a man of weak passion if, on the occasion of a coitus, his desire for the act is not intense, his movements during the act slow and his semen scanty, and if he squirms at the scratching or biting administered by the other partner, denoting that he cannot bear her warm embrace. A man whose sexual impulse, semen and ability to bear scratching's and bites are middling is called moderately passionate. A man with an intense desire, a large stock of semen and an extreme toleration for scratching's and bites is termed intensely passionate.

By similar standards, too, women are divided into weak, moderate and intense according to the relative strength of their passion.

In this classification also, union between a Weak male and a weak female, between a moderate male and a moderate female, or between an intense male and an intense female is considered the best.

There are six kinds of unequal union according to the degree of passion:

(1) Union between a weak male and a moderate female

(2) Union between a weak male and an intense female

(3) Union between a moderate male and a weak female

(4) Union between a moderate male and an intense female

(5) Union between an intense male and a weak female

(6) Union between an intense male and a moderate female

Similarly, men and women are divided into three categories from the standpoint of DURATION OF COITUS:

the short-timed, the medium-timed and the long-timed.

Here also, union between short-timed partners, between medium timed partners or between long-timed partners is considered the best. There may be six other kinds of union in which the parties are not evenly matched.

There is, however, difference of opinion over the question whether women can be properly classified according to the time it would take them to reach orgasm during coitus.

 Auddalaki, an ancient authority, is of Opinion that women are constitutionally unable to derive the same kind of pleasure as men experience before and during ejaculation, since the former emit no semen. He argues that the vaginal cavity of woman is naturally inhabited by countless parasites which give rise to a sensation of itching in the vagina and that the rhythmic penial friction during coitus relieves this itching. If this relief is withheld, a woman becomes hysterical. He further contends that since the process of relief of that itching, coupled with such pleasurable by-play as kissing, etc., creates a feeling of voluptuousness and the woman appears to feel a sort of pleasure, and that a woman's sensation of pleasure begins from the point where the relief of the itching begins, i.e. from the moment of penetration. But as a man's pleasure lies in the process of seminal ejaculation, the pleasure felt by the respective parties in the act is different in character from each other. Therefore, there cannot be any classification of women according to intensity and duration of coitus.

If in view of this hypothesis, it be that man and woman cannot each realise the quality and character of the pleasure felt by the other, how, in that case, can one state definitely that the feeling experienced by a woman are different from those experienced by a man?

Well, says Auddalaki, it is understood from the fact that a man, having effected penetration, ceases action when he wants to, without waiting for the woman; if a woman felt the pleasure of ejaculation, she could break off by withdrawing her organ as soon as she had ejaculated. But a woman does not break off before her mate has had his pleasure to the argument that a long-timed, male partner is particularly dear to women while a short-time male, being unable to satisfy women, is hated by them, thus showing that they reveal their passion and loathing, and also there occurs the discharge of fluid in the woman, Auddalaki replies that a long coitus is preferred because it relieves the itching: that is what their affection and dislike prove and not the fact of their ejaculation like men.

In this connection Vabhravya observes: "The young woman begins to feel voluptuous pleasure from the start of the coitus but the man has his pleasure at the close. This is an observed fact. If it be not true that women achieve a secretion, how can they conceive?" That is, women, like men, secrete a fluid from the start of the communion and attain the satisfaction of an active desire like men, and the difference being that women's gratification continues from the start but that men's begins with the process of ejaculation. "If the theory of relief of itching be true," remarks Vabhravya," it cannot be reconciled to the fact that the female has more or less equanimity when she is approached, that she is roused more and more as she is pawed, scratched, embraced and kissed and that she desires to withdraw from coitus when she has experienced an orgasm. It. therefore, cannot be true. the motion of the potter's wheel and the turner's lathe, a woman's passion is weak at first, gathers force gradually and finally attains the maximum intensity. Since cessation is desired when orgasm has taken place, passion disappears after it."

The conclusion, therefore, is that woman, like man, experiences acute pleasure in coitus and emits the seminal fluid at the end of the act.

When a male and a female are of the same species of beings, comments Vatsyayana, and when they engage in the same act (sexual union) with the same end in view (pleasure from ejaculation), how can their action, be of two different kinds.? That is possible only when the respective roles and the feelings roused are of two different kinds. Why are the roles different? Because they are so designed by Nature. Man is the active agent and woman the receptacle. Their actions are, therefore, different and naturally their feelings are different. The man considers it his role to apply himself to the woman for experiencing his pleasure and the woman thinks it her role to be applied to for experiencing her pleasure. Thus it is that they engage each other in a sexual union. But can the result be different because the respective roles are not the same? No. There is a reason for the difference in role. It is illogical to suppose that the experience of pleasure must be different because the active agent and the recipient have different roles, for they belong to the same species and are interdependent upon each other for the proper performance of coitus. Therefore, the pleasure is the same for man and woman both in respect of its nature and its duration

It may still be objected that such common experience is possible when several agents jointly execute a common task

But here man and woman appear to be serving different interests (since the man ejaculates the seminal fluid and the other receives the secretion), so how can they derive the same pleasure?

Yes, admits Vatsyayana, several interests can be better served at the same time as in the charging of two rams, in the impact of two hard-shelled fruits or in the tussle between two wrestlers. But they both are active agents, while in sexual congress one is apparently active and the other apparently passive. There is, however, no fundamental difference between them, for they are both equally indispensable for one complete act of intercourse. Really neither party is passive or indirect, they are both equally active. The final conclusion, therefore, is that both experience the same intensity of pleasure. Therefore, the male should make such love-play, i.e., kissing, embracing, etc., as rouses the passion of the female beforehand and makes her eager for having a coition."

Now, since it is established that both man and woman attain an equal climax of pleasure, there are nine kinds of union according to the dimensions of the organs, nine according the duration of coitus and nine according to the degree of passion. The combination of all these produce innumerable kinds of union.

Vatsyayana observes that all the three factors being given due consideration, appropriate love-play should be practised so that there may be complete pleasure in spite of the disparities that may exist.

The passion of the male at the first intercourse is intense and his duration short, but in subsequent unions the reverse will be the case. With the female, however, it is the contrary, for at the first time her passion is weak and she takes a long time to achieve orgasm, but on subsequent occasions her passion is stronger and she is more easily roused and satisfied. It very often happens that the male ejaculates the seminal fluid before the female has discharged the fluid that marks an orgasm. It is pointed out, therefore, that the act should be so managed that the female reaches the acme of delight before the male has reached the peak of his pleasure.

Women with soft parts are easily satisfied; and those who are not naturally endowed with soft parts can, by means of kisses, embraces and manual caresses of the vulva, be softened and easily satisfied. All preceptors agree on this point.

All the above instructions as to technique, being very brief, will only be understood by those proficient in the Four categories of Science of Love. For the edification of sexual gratification the lay public, Vatsyayana hereinafter sets forth in detail the technique of sexual union. Experts in the laws of Kama (sexual passion) hold that there are four kinds of satisfaction:

(1)   That arising out of habitual practice of a certain action;

(2) That arising out of the imagination of sexual union through the commission of certain actions resembling, but different from, union;

(3) That arising out of sexual union with persons not from intended;

(4) That arising out of the direct perceptions of all the senses.

(1)   The manifestation of pleasure from the constant and continued performance of an action connected with the five senses is called habitual satisfaction, that obtained from hunting, drinking, etc. being instances of this type.

(2)   The pleasure obtained through the mental contemplation of an act not habitually done is called imaginary satisfaction; so also is the satisfaction obtained through mouth congress or fellatio (in which the mouth becomes the venue of ejaculation) practised by eunuchs and perverse women and also through kisses, embraces, etc. for it is born of the sensation of touch.

(3)   When a man or a women receives the embraces of a

woman or a man respectively, pretending that the partner is not the person that he or she really is but somebody else who was one's object of desire, that is another variety of assumed satisfaction.

(4) The immediate satisfaction directly received through the senses as the result of pleasurable contacts is called sensuous satisfaction. This is immediate and is understood by everybody; as the content of satisfaction is the highest in this, this is the principal form of satisfaction and the foregoing three kinds are but divisions of it. All these different kinds of pleasure should be properly considered. Whatever the character of the desire that demands pleasurable satisfaction, one should proceed to meet it in the approved manner.

The idea is that in this kind of satisfaction the union is with the person really desired, there is satisfaction of all the senses and union is major and real. The scope of the four categories of gratification requires elucidation. In category (1) there is passion in the male. There is also the habitual gratification by coitus without discrimination as to the identity of the female partner, as in the case of a habitual whoremonger. In category (2) there is no coitus but satisfaction sexual desire from the practice of perversities like fellatio, pederasty, of masturbation and sadistic and masochistic behaviour. In category (3) there is coitus, but not with the person who has excited passion. As for example, a man has a violent desire for possessing a woman whom he cannot approach. He, therefore, relieves his passion on another approachable woman, making believe during coitus that she is the woman desired. In category (4) there is union with the woman desired. There is coitus and also other by-plays. The last category combines relief of an overmastering passion as ín (1) satisfaction of minor sexual impulses through kisses, embraces etc., as in (2) and the belief that the woman is the woman desired as worked up in (3).

CHAPTER 12
THE ART OF EMBRACES

EARLIER preceptors have remarked that sexual union has sixty-four accessories, since one complete act of Coitus comprises sixty-four minor actions. They also say that since the Science of Love rests on the sixty-four methods of love-play, that also has sixty-four branches. Coincidentally, the fine arts are sixty-four in number. They, too, are integral parts of the complete act of sexual intercourse. Moreover, this has been corroborated in the portion of the Rig Veda called Dashatayi. Since this science has particular relation to the Rig Veda and has also been incorporated in it by sage Panchala, some are of opinion that the priests have introduced the name sixty-four" for it.

According to the followers of Vabhravya, there are eight steps of a sexual act, namely:

I.   Embrace;

II.   Kissing;

III. Scratching with finger-nails;

IV.   Biting and bruising with the teeth;

V.   Attitude in coitus;

VI.   Stroking and making various inarticulate sounds;

VII. Reversed coitus (woman playing the part of man);

VIII. Coitus in ore (fellatio).

Each of these have approximately eight varieties.

They are, therefore, about sixty-four in number, according to Vabhravya. Of the eight divisions mentioned some have more than eight varieties each and some have less. For example, beating, murmuring, intromission and novel attitudes in coitus form new subdivisions within divisions, as has often been said. Like the words " seven divisions, as has often been said. leaved tree" and five-coloured" offerings to deities, the word "sixty-four" is only approximate.

Of this accessory technique, the kiss is usually given after the embrace. Therefore, the EMBRACE being the first step, will now be discussed. There may be two modes of embracing: the first relates to a woman who has never been embraced before and the second to one who has already experienced it (either from the present lover or from previous lovers). For the edification of lovers ignorant of the modes of embracing inexperienced girls the technique is explained below.

The embrace is a mark of affection and is generally of four kinds, namely:

I. SLIGHT CONTACT (Sprishtaka)- In this kind of embrace the two bodies merely touch each other without pressure. This is employed when the beloved woman is in front of one, yet cannot be embraced. To show his desire for her the man passes by her side on some pretext and brushes lightly against her body with his own in such manner that any other person present there may not suspect that he has deliberately done this.

2. BREAST-PRESSURE EMBRACE (Viddhaka)-In this kind of embrace it is the woman who takes the initiative. The woman finds her beloved seated or standing in a secluded place, moves there under the pretence of picking up something, and presses his body with her breasts. The man in return clasps her with his arms around her. (This may be either from the front or from behind.)

Both these kinds of embrace are applicable to couples who have known each other for some time, but are not yet intimate.

3. RUBBING EMBRACE (Udghrishtaka)-This is the kind of embrace in which the man and the woman press and rub one's body against that of another slowly and for a long time. This applies to meetings in the darkness or in the midst of a crowd or even in a secluded place. If both the parties are actively employed in the embrace, it is called udghrishtaka. but when only one party is ally it is called ghrishtaka.

4. PRESSIVE-RUBBING EMBRACE (Piditaka) - This is a more forcible variety of the rubbing embrace. During the embrace one of the couple either forces the other against a wall or a pillar and exerts pressure or simply clasps the other tightly and makes a rubbing movement of the body.

These two latter forms of embrace are peculiar to those couples who have avowed their love for each other by hints and signs.

When lovers meet for sexual intercourse the following

four kinds of Intimate embraces are used:

1. TWINING OF A CREEPER (Lata-veshtitaka)-The woman clings to her lover who is standing, with her arms twined around him as a creeper twines around a tree. trunk. She raises her mouth, looks lovingly at him and draws down the face of her lover for meeting in a kiss. Or, clasping the lover's body, she makes low sounds and looks either down at the tips of her breasts or aside at any other pleasing object. This embrace is meant to inflame the desire of the man.

2. CLIMBING OF A TREE (Vrikshadhirudhaka)-In this style of intimate embrace the woman puts one of her feet on the foot of her lover who is standing, while the other leg is twined around one of his thighs, which causes the friction of her pudenda against those of her partner. Or she passes one arm round his back and with the other draws down his shoulder and makes low rapturous sounds and sounds of cooing. At the same time she also tries to raise her body higher, as if by climbing up the lover's body, in order to have a kiss.

These two intimate embraces are for lovers in a standing attitude and their purpose is to rouse the passion for sexual intercourse to its highest pitch.

3. GUMMED-UP CLASP (Teela-tandulaka- The mixture of sesame seed with rice')-The lovers lie on their side face to face and embrace each other closely so that the one lying on the left side passes the left hand under the left thigh the right side of the other and vice versa. of the one rests upon the right thigh of the other, while the right thigh is raised upon the other's left so that friction be continued with of the pudenda may greater facility.

4. COMPLETE-FUSION CLASP (Kshira-nivaka- The fusion of milk and water)-The woman faces the lover, sitting on his lap; or, if they are lying on the bed, the man strongly clasps the body of the woman. They are so beside themselves with the blinding urge for coitus that they want to enter into each other's body without caring whether their bones will break under the pressure.

These two embraces should be practised at the stage when the membrum of the male is erect and the woman's vagina is lubricated with the pre-coital secretion but penetration has not yet taken place.

The embraces mentioned above have been discussed by Vabhravya. But still more intimate embraces have been described by Suvarnanabha. These are useful during the act of coitus. They are stated to give even greater pleasure than the eight embraces recommended by Vabhravya which have been mentioned above.

1. THIGH PINCERS (Urupaguhana) - One of the two lovers will clasp with his or her thighs either one or both thighs of the other and will exert pressure, as if with a pair of closing pincers. The partner whose thighs are the fleshier will take the active part. This is practised with the couple lying sidewise face to face.

2. HIP-THIGH EMBRACE (Jaghanupaguhana)—The man lies on his back and the woman mounts upon him. She presses her pubes upon that of the man, , loosens her hair and

seeks to administer nail-scratches, bites, strokes and kisses to the lover.

3. EMBRACE OF THE BREASTS (Stanalingana) The woman presses her breasts on the chest of her lover, throwing the whole weight of her body. In this way the man will experience great pleasure from the soft pervasive touch of the woman's flesh. This may be done in a sit ting posture or when both are lying on their sides or when the man is in the supine position.

4. EMBRACE OF THE FOREHEADS (Lalalika) -The woman lies either upon the supine man or faces him lying side by side. She glues her lips to his in a kiss, her eyes look into his eyes and she touches his forehead with hers several times, so that her lover's brow is smeared with the colours with which her forehead is decorated.

Some are of the opinion that rubbing or squeezing, which gives extreme pleasure through the skin, the muscles and the bones, is a kind of embrace. In the opinion of Vatsyayana, however, rubbing is quite distinct from the embrace, for it is employed on different occasions and for different purposes. Moreover, rubbing is not always pleasant to both the parties. It is pointed out that the various forms of the embrace are practised either immediately before or during sexual communion, but rubbing which includes also massaging and squeezing-is useful at other times too. Again, when lovers embrace each other, both are inflamed with passion; but rubbing or massaging is effective with a man when it is administered by a woman and vice versa. It is true, indeed, that both massaging and the embrace make their appeal felt through the medium of the sense of touch, but they are not of the same kind. If they are so, then kissing also should be classed as a kind of embrace, for here too the appeal is through the same sense of touch.

In conclusion it has been said: "Even those who discuss the various methods of the embrace are smitten with an overpowering desire for sexual congress. What need is there to speak of those who would practise it? It is likely that there are other voluptuous embraces that have not been discussed in this treatise but that are either known to people or are possible methods in love-making. Since their object is to increase excitement in coition, these also should be practised. The rules and processes laid down in the Science of Love are of value only in stimulating a moderate desire; but when the wheel of passion has once begun to roll (i.e., when sexual passion has become over powering) instructions on methods and order of love-play become superfluous."

CHAPTER 13
THE ART AND TECHNIQUE OF KISSING

AFTER the embrace (not, of course, the intimate and the more intimate varieties of it) the lovers should proceed to kissing and other more passionate forms of love-play. A question may arise as to forms of love-play the order in which kissing, scratching and biting should be performed. Vatsyayana, therefore, definitely declares that all the three may be performed in the order that is suitable to the occasion and to the particular liking of the parties concerned, for they are indulged in under the influence of a powerful sexual excitement. But they should be done generally before the major union takes place. Stroking and making of various erotic sounds should, however, take place during coitus. Since all these are designed to increase passion, it is not rational to assign a particular order to each form of love-play, for the coital urge in extremely passionate persons does not wait for order or time. These processes of sexual caress do not acquire definite value at the first union of lovers. Therefore, one or another process—but not all of them, should be applied on a girl whose confidence has been newly won, for the coital urge in woman is weak at first. Later, with the increase of passion all the processes should be employed rapidly, safely or definitely so that the partner becomes heated and impatient to engage in coitus.

Referring to the technique of the KISS, Vatsyayana observes that it should be given on the forehead, the fore locks, the cheeks, the eyes, the male's chest, the breasts, The technique of the lips and the interior of the mouth. the kiss

Among the people of the Lata country (Southern Gujerat) there is also the custom of kissing the vulva, the armpits, and the region above the pubes. There are also other spots for kissing that are traditional to particular localities and peoples. By custom and prevalent suggestion, they have acquired value in conveying and communicating passion to the woman partner. Vatsyayana is of the opinion that such local customs should be observed in those localities where they are prevalent and in those cases where the woman being wooed may belong to them, but should not be extended to all cases.

The KISS consists in the touching, by lips curved in the shape of a bud, of suitable parts of another's body. The varieties of the kiss are due to the various parts of the body touched by the lips. Among these, again, the kiss on the mouth takes the leading role. For a girl inexperienced in sexual practice and not yet possessing enough confidence in her lover to allow him to possess her, there are three forms of the lip kiss:

(1) The LIMITED KISS (Nimitaka)-The girl, persuaded or forced gently to give the lover a kiss, touches with her lips those of the partner, but does not attempt to press or suck them.

(2) The TREMBLING KISS (Sphuritaka)-The man takes the lower lip of the woman between his own lips and she sets aside her bashfulness a little and wishes to res pond. This being the first response, her action is hesitant; she is alternately forward and reticent. She tries to take her lips away and not allow the man to keep his lips fixed on hers. She does not, however, actually take away her lips for, should the lover try to draw away his lips, she at once fixes them in place by pressing them with her own.

This kiss is so named on account of the trembling of the girl's lips.

(3) The EXPLORATORY KISS (Ghattitaka)-This represents further progress by the woman. In the form of kissing she covers the eyes of her lover with the palm her and shuts her own eyes. Then she lightly takes the tip of his lower lip between her own lips and caresses the imprisoned lip with a rotatory movement of her tongue. This is so named because the girl's lip executes a probing movement.

There are five other kinds of the lip-kiss in which the man is generally the active partner:

(1) When the man and the woman face each other directly, the seizure of the lower lip of the woman by the lips of the man is called the STRAIGHT KISS (Sama).

(2) When the face of one is screwed a little towards that of the other and the lower lip of the other is held with lips pressed in the form of a 0, it is called an OBLIQUE KISS (Vakra).

(3) When the one implants a kiss on the lips of the other after turning the latter's face towards one by holding the other's head and chin, it is called the REVOLVING KISS (Udbhranta).

(4) If in the above position the lips of one party press forcibly upon those of the other, the result will be a PRESSED KISS (Avapidita). If in such a kiss both press their lips upon each other's, it will be a GENTLY PRESSED KISS (Suddhavapidita) and if the pressure is exerted also with the lip of the tongue, such a kiss is called a SUCKING KISS or DRINKING THE LIP (Chushana or adhara-pana).

(5) When the lower lip, taken between the thumb and the forefinger, is pressed into the shape of a ball and then, after being touched with the tongue, is pressed and sucked by the lips of the other partner without being bitten, it is called a SUPER-PRESSED KISS (Akrishta).

Having described the various kinds of the lip-kiss, the first three kinds of which are given by virgins and the next five given and received by both parties, Vatsyayana recommends as the next step the laying of wagers in the form of a competition as to who will get hold of the of other first so as to heighten their sexual excitement.

The couple should fix a wager and then fall to kissing each other with gusto. and the partner who succeeds in capturing the lips of the other in a pressed or super-pressed kiss wins the wager. Since such a game cannot by very nature be a drawn one. either party must win, and it may well happen that the man becomes the winner. In that case the female partner in the contest will certainly pretend to cry and be on the verge of tears affecting to be painfully hurt in the lips. She will shake her fingers al him, threaten him and keep him off by pushing him away. If the lover attempts now only to embrace her and kiss her lips—which he is certain to do—she bites his lips; II she does not succeed in doing that, she turns away from him and disputes with him that his alleged win is either a fluke or obtained by unfair means. The lover, of course, similarly insists that she has been beaten. She then demands a fresh wager. And should she lose the wager again, she again appears to be very much put out. Or if the woman be a clever one, she diverts the attention of her lover by interesting conversation or a faked quarrel. As soon as she finds her lover off his guard or asleep, she imprisons her lover's lip within hers and so holds it between her teeth that he may not release it. When she has caught and held his lip, she keeps it fast so that it may not slip away. Then she laughs, shouts, threatens to bite his lip, calls out for his or her friends, throws herself upon her lover with jerks and sudden gestures, dances gleefully and taunts him on his so-called defeat, moving her eye-brows and rolling her eyes. All this ends in renewed embraces and caressing.

In this sham contest of kissing the part of the lover is to emulate the woman and be revenged upon her in an exactly similar manner. The game involves, beside embracing and kissing, nail-scratching, biting and stroking. It is evident, however, that only men and women of an extremely passionate nature can engage in such a game of kissing and that persons of weak passion will be unable to stand the violent and intense excitement that attends and follows it.

In this contest of kisses, as also in the pressed and super-pressed varieties of the kiss, when the women sucks the lower lip of her lover, he should take her upper lip and suck it in. This is called the CONCURRENT OR RESPONSIVE KISS, also known as KISS OF THE UPPER LIPS (Uttara-Chumbita).

When one of them takes both the lips of the other between his or her own and sucks them with both lips. making a sound as of whistling, it is called the CUPPING KISS (Samputaka). When it is the woman that holds his lower lip the man finds it delicious to suck her upper lip, but when it is the man who drinks the woman's lower lip she can only enjoy sucking his upper lip when he has not grown moustaches or is clean shaved. For, it is explained, the suction of bristles into the mouth is repugnant to women. While engaged in such a prolonged kiss, if the lovers brush each other's teeth and tongue with the tips of their tongues and, thrusting them still farther, one licks the palate of the other and the other partner in turn licks one's tongue and palate, it is called the BATTLE OF THE TONGUES (Jihva-yuddha). This explains inner mouth, teeth, tongue or palate kissing and represents the conquest of the lips and the teeth and also the surrender thereof by the other party.

In respect of other parts of the body, there are four kinds of kisses :

(1) Kisses on the pelvic rump, on the navel and on the chest are called BALANCED KISSES (Sama), being neither too forcible nor body

too light. (2) Kisses on the breasts, the cheeks and the vulva are called FORCIBLE KISSES (Pidita) as a considerable amount of passion goes into such a form of kissing.

(3) Kisses on the breasts downwards to the waist may also be called WORSHIPFUL KISSES (Anchita) when they are given in a chaste frame of mind.

(4) Kisses on the forehead and the eyes are called MILD OF AFFECTIONATE KISSES (Mridu) as they are 800 ally given in a delicately affectionate mood.

Kisses also take on different names according to the circumstances in which they are given. Thus when a woman looks at the face of her lover while he is a sleep and kisses it to show her own impulse or desire, it is called the PASSION-AROUSING kiss or the kiss that kindles love for this kiss arouses the passion of the female to a burning heat. The kiss that is given while the man is occupied in other indifferent matters (e.g., business), to end a quarrel between them, to divert his interest from something when he is looking intently in another direction or to interrupt him while about to drop off to sleep, is called the STARTER Or DIVERTING KISS. The kiss given by the man on returning home late at night to her beloved who is pretending to be asleep in bed, in order to show his desire, is called the SIGNALLING KISS. The idea is that the woman may feign to be asleep at the time of her lover's arrival so that she may know whether he desires a union. The kiss given on, or blown to the shadow or reflection of the other on a mirror or on lighted wall or on the surface of water is called the REFLECTING KISS or a kiss showing intention. The kiss and embrace given to a child, a portrait or a statue of the beloved in her own presence is called the TRANSFERRED KISS. This applies to the case in which the beloved has been untouched and un spoken to before. This kiss is a hint to show that the man is yearning to approach her for sexual relationship.

In a similar manner and with the object of communicating her desire, the woman kisses the fingers of the lover's hand at night at a theatre or at a social gathering of relations. The female may also kiss the toes of the man when he is lying on the bed beside her. A man is forbidden to kiss the toes of the woman of his desire, for the sight of such abject subjection may induce a woman to give herself up for the sexual act out of pity without feeling the necessary passion. When a woman, while gently rubbing with her palm the thighs of the supine man (i.e. while massaging her lover's body), places her face on his thighs as if she were sleepy and kisses his thigh or great toe so as to inflame his passion the kiss is called the INTERROGATORY or DEMON STRATIVE KISS. By this the woman conveys to him her love for him, but does not know how he feels about her.

When a woman gives a passionate kiss denoting her desire for sexual union or a simple INTERROGATORY kiss the man should respond similarly. If the woman goads him or kisses him, he should goad or kiss her with equal fervour. Then alone can the act produce full joy and satisfaction.

CHAPTER 14
THE ART OF MARKING AND SCRATCHING WITH THE NAILS

KISSING in the manner described in the foregoing chapter will serve to awaken in man and woman the desire for sexual intercourse. This desire should be increased further by the application of NAIL-MARKING or SCRATCHES. This consists of friction on the skin of the body with the finger nails with the increase of sexual excitement. It should be practised on the body of the beloved

(1)   on the occasion of the first sexual intimacy,

(2) on the return of the lover from abroad (i.e., after prolonged absence),

(3) on set ting out on a long journey,

(4) on the mollification of an angry mistress or wife and

(5) when the woman has been intoxicated with wines and spirits. Those who are not of an extremely passionate temperament should not practise this on every occasion. For the weakly passionate and the moderately passionate classes of men and women such practice should be resorted to only occasionally. For a man who has been either intoxicated or coaxed out of dis pleasure into an amatory frame of mind and also for men and women of an extremely passionate temperament, nail scratching should be performed on every occasion of sexual intercourse.

Similarly DENTAL MARKS should also be applied according to the intensity of excitement of the couple or on those who are full of passion and to whom the practice is agreeable.

Erotic bite-marks are defined as marks made with the teeth that are administered out of ecstasy of coital passion. If the ecstasy of passion is not very intense, the significant spots of the partner's body should only be touched with the teeth and not pressed. If both the partners are of a weakly passionate temperament, this technique should not be employed at all.

NAIL MARKS can either follow definite patterns or may consist of random scratching's. There are eight recognised patterns or forms produced by nail-marks:

(1) Sounding or limited pressure, (2) Half-moon: (3) Circle, (4) Line, (5) Tiger's claw, (6) Peacock's foot; (7) Leaping hare; (8) Leaf of a lotus.

Random marking can be of three kinds according to the dimensions and depth of scratching:

(1) Light or small, (2) Medium or middling, (3) Large or heavy.

The following are places of the body that are recommended for nail-marks:

(1)   The sides including and up to the arm-pits;

(2)   The female breasts and the male chest;

(3)   The neck and the throat; (

(4)   The back;

(5)   The middle part of the body, including the waist, the buttock, the lower abdomen and the pubic region;

(6) The thighs.

Suvarnanabha, however, observes that in the frenzy of excitement any part of the body is liable to be scratched, and the greater the intensity of passion the more the irregularity of markings.

But these markings serve a significant purpose. Some of these are made on those parts of the body which are not usually covered by the dress.

These markings are visible to friends, whose curiosity as to the last night's enjoyments serve to kindle in the man fresh or woman pleasant memories and a desire for a experience of the rapturous delights associated with these markings.

The finger-nails of the left hand of men and women of an intensely passionate temperament should be long and furnished with two or three ridges like the blade of a saw. They should be trimmed afresh frequently. The moderately passionate and the weakly passionate people will have nails of a different shape. The former's nails will have one ridge only fashioned in the shape of a grain of corn and will be less sharp, while those of the latter will be shaped like a half moon and will have an entirely blunt edge. The characteristics of good finger-nails are that they shall have tinted lines on them, shall be of a smooth surface, shall be bright and shall not crumble in spots. They shall be well-grown, soft of touch, glossy of appearance and pleasing to look at.

The citizens of Gaud (north-western Bengal and eastern Bihar) have long and decorative nails that are very much liked by women. They are not experts at scratching.

The people of the Deccan have short, hard and businesslike nails which are capable of executing all forms of scratching, as the people are of a passionate temperament. The people of Maharashtra (the country between the Narmada river and the Karnata district), who are of both mild and strong passion, have medium-sized nails which can do both light and heavy scratching in an expert manner.

When a person possessing medium-sized nails places them upon the jaw or the lower lip or upon the mount of the breasts of the other party so that the fingers spread apart and are pressed slowly as to pinch the part just a little and then are drawn together with a gradually closing motion so lightly as to make no scratch-mark, the result will be a Pleasant tingling sensation from the touch of the nails which will cause all the hair near the spot to stand erect.

Now the action is repeated more rapidly. When the nails close in at the tip of the breasts or the centre of the lips. they will make a sound by reason of one clashing upon another. This is called the SOUNDING or LIMITED PRESSURE SCRATCH (Achchuritaka). This is mainly applied on the breasts.

This style of scratching is also applicable to all such parts of the body of the woman who is being wooed as can be rubbed or massaged, also to the head, when it needs scratching, the sites of boils, pustules, etc. It is also applied to fluster and frighten young girls who, out of shyness, will not permit any advances. This method of scratching is applicable in all circumstances and to all types of men and women.

When the nails are pressed on the neck and the breasts in a semi-circular curve in such a manner as to leave a bruise-mark, the figure so made is called a HALF-MOON (Ardhachandraka).

When two such semi-circular marks are impressed opposite to each other, the correspondent ends joining, it is called a CIRCLE (MANDALA). This mark may also be made on the pubic region and below the navel, around the sacral dimples (i.e., the depressions above the buttocks) and on the hip-joints. Short semi-circular or circular marks may be made anywhere on the body.

Curved bruise-lines radiating upwards from the nipples of the breasts are called the TIGER'S CLAW (Vyaghranakha). Marks made around the breasts with the five nails that con verge on the nipples are called the PEA COCK'S FOOT (Mayurapadaka).

This nail-mark is made by putting the thumb below the nipples of the breasts and the other fingers above the tip and then by drawing them together. The thumb is placed just below the nipple and the other fingers are placed above it, touching one another nipple and the latter are drawn towards the tip of the peacock's leaving a scratch resembling the outline of a talon.

When the five nails, touching one another, are placed around the nipple of a woman who regards the practice of sexual union with pride and are forcibly driven into the flesh around the nipple, the mark thus caused is called the LEAPING HARE (Shashaplutaka).

When nail-marks made on the breasts and the waist of a woman resemble a leaf of the lotus it is called the The Leaf of a LOTUS LEAF (Utpalapatraka). That on Lotus

the breasts should be in the shape of one leaf. The waist should be nail-marked with a number of such scratches resembling a garland of lotus leaves.

Scratches on the thighs or breasts of the woman in the form of three or four lines that meet one another is called the TOKEN OF REMEMBRANCE (Smaraniyaka), as it is made by a lover going abroad so that the sight or feel of The Token of the scratch may remind her of the absent Remembrance lover. If the separation is to be very long, there will be four such lines; if long, three lines and if short, only one or two lines according to the period of separation. A woman can also make such marks on her lover's body.

Nail-scratches may be made also in many other forms. Though only eight principally recognised forms have been Application of noted above, the preceptors in the Science other scratch of Love recognise that there may be in marks

E numerable forms of marking and that there may be an infinite variety in its technique and practice. No one, in these circumstances, can define all the kinds and varieties of nail-marks that do actually exist, but it is pointed out that adepts in the eight principal forms will be able at their will to design and execute any number of scratch-marks as occasion demands. For, it has been found that reciprocity in the sexual act is promoted by variety and novelty in the technique of love-play, of which scratching constitutes an important part. Even the accomplished courtesan, who receives all men with a professional welcome and indifference of heart, craves the embraces of a lover adept in the art of scratching, just as beau accomplished in the same art desires the pleasures of embraces from a courtesan who knows fully the art of giving complete sexual satisfaction. When even such rude acts as archery and fighting are improved by the use of novel methods, can there be any doubt that novelty or variety is necessary in love since passion is increase the variety of caresses ?

The novel forms of nail marks, however, should not be made on a married mistress, for these may betray her secret love affairs. But especially designed marks with the nails may be made on her private parts for her remembrance and to make her yearn for her secret lover. The old moribund love of a woman becomes refreshed and strong anew when she perceives the marks made by her lover on the private parts of her body, even though such marks may be old and almost worn out. If there be no marks to remind a person of the beauty, youthfulness and attractive qualities of the beloved, then love is liable to lessen and decay through neglect. Even a man who looks from a distance at a young woman with marks of nails on her breasts instantly conceives a strong desire for her though she may be a total stranger to him. Also, the sight of a male body with marks of nails and teeth on it very often excites a woman's desire even though she may have hardened her heart by penance. Marking with nails and teeth are the most powerful methods of increasing the erotic passion.

CHAPTER 15
THE ART OF EROTIC BITING

All parts of the body that can be kissed are also the parts that can be bitten with the teeth with the exception of the upper lip, the tongue and the eyes, The possible parts include the forehead, the lower lip, the neck, the cheeks, the female breasts, the male chest and, according to the custom of people of the Lata (southern Gujerat) country, the hip-joints or the joints of the thighs, the armpits, and the pelvic rump. The latter however, are not universally recognised as parts fit for being either kissed or bitten." The qualities of a good set of teeth are as follows: They should be even, smooth and bright, easily tinted with colouring matter like betels neither too big nor too small (.e., well-proportioned), closely set and with sharp ends. Teeth that have decayed (carious), are with chapped and broken enamel. have rough surfaces, are unevenly and loosely set, are either too large or too small, and are set apart from one another, are of a defective quality.

The following are the different types of biting:

(1) The Hidden bite;

(2) The Canine or Swollen bite;

(3) The Point or Spot,

(4) The Spot-chain;

(5) The Coral;

(6) The Coral chain;

(7) The Broken cloud;

(8) The Boar's bite.

Soft pressure with one of the principal teeth that leaves only a faint red mark and denotes the first awakening of the sexual desire is called the HIDDEN BITE (Gudhaka).

When such a bite is executed with pressure so that the spot bitten swells up into a temporary weal it is called the CANINE or SWOLLEN BITE (Uchchhunaka). The lower lip is the spot on which the Hidden bite, the Canine bite and the Point are made. The Canine and the Coral are also made on the cheeks. The left cheek is preferred for kissing and biting, which decorate it (the left cheek) like an ear-ring.

When a portion of the body is taken between one's lower lip and upper front teeth and pressure is exerted again and again, it leaves a bright red contusion mark on the skin. This is called the CORAL (Pravala-mani). Several such red marks made in the fashion of a chain called the CORAL CHAIN (Manimala).

When a very small portion of the skin is held between lower front tooth and the upper lip and is press leaves a spot-like mark. This is called the SPOT or POINT (Vindu), and such marks made in a series with all the front teeth of the lower set together are called the SPOT CHAIN (Vindu-mala).

Both the CORAL CHAIN and the SPOT CHAIN are to be impressed on the neck and the throat, the chest including the arm-pits, and the hip-joints only, for the skin of these parts is thin. The SPOT CHAIN can also be applied to the forehead and the thighs.

When the female breasts are pressed with the two entire sets of teeth, a circular mark of unequal breadth (on account of the difference in breadth of the biting surface of teeth) is left. This is called the BROKEN CLOUD (Khanda bhraka). When a small portion of the skin of the breast or shoulders is taken between the teeth and chewed and then another portion is taken and so on, it leaves a long unbroken line of scarlet weal's. This is called the BOAR'S BITE (Varahacharvitaka). These two are peculiar to persons of an intensely passionate temperament.

When figures representing one of these scratch-marks or bite-marks are executed on leaves of flowers fashioned for ornamenting the brow (tilaka), on ear-rings and crowns made of flowers, on betel leaves or on tamala leaves that serve for billets doux and sent to the lover or lady-love in secret they are called CODE APPEALS signifying the desire for an intimate enjoyment. These marks, which indicate the different stages of the sexual passion are in these cases designed to show the stage of desire reached by the sender and are meant as requests for an assignation.

CHAPTER 16
LOCAL CUSTOMS AND PRACTICES IN LOVE-PLAY

WHEN a woman is to be made to reciprocate in the sexual act the methods of love-play peculiar to the locality to which she belongs should be used. When a woman wants a man to respond to her passion she should similarly make use of the local forms of love-play to which her man is respond to her passion a accustomed.

Women of Madhyadesha (the Ganges-Jumna doab). being of decent habits almost like the Aryans are fond of the embrace but dislike unclean methods of love-play like kissing, pressing with nails and biting.

Women of Vahlika (northern region about Bactria) and Avantipura kingdoms (modern Ujjain) also are averse to kissing and similar practices, but they are excessively fond of coitus in unusual attitudes.

Women of Eastern Malava (east of Ujjain) and the Abhira country (land around Kurukshetra, etc.) very much like being embraced, kissed, scratched, bit, sucked, stroked, etc., so long as these are not vigorous enough to cause bruises.

Women inhabiting the Indus basin (the Punjab and Sind) are very fond of fellatio and cunnilinctus. Those of the Aparanta kingdom on the shores of the Western Sea (northern Konkan) and those of the Lata country (southern Gujerat) are, indeed, of a passionate temperament; they can tolerate stroking's and sounds indicative of furious passion (sheetkrita).

Women of Stri-Rajya (a state on the northern reaches near Vahlika) and those of Koshala (Oudh) are quick of passion. They like to be hard beaten during sexual inter course and, to satisfy their lust, often resort to artificial appliances resembling the membrum virile in shape.

Women of the Andhra kingdom (northern part of the Madras Presidency) are by nature mild and have tender bodies; they are fond of frequent sexual contact but can not tolerate being hard beaten. But they are not of decent tastes and do not follow clean methods. (That is, their conduct is neither artistic nor delicate).

Women of Maharashtra (the country between the Narmada and Karnata kingdom) are fond of practising the sixty-four arts; they love to speak obscene and side words and to be spoken to in the same way in the matter of sexual union, they assume the superior position and take the man by force.

Women of Nagara (modern Jaipur State) are of the same nature as the women of Maharashtra but they practice the sixty-four arts and use obscene language only in private, unlike the latter who do so in public.

Women of the Dravida kingdom (south of the Karnata country), as soon as they are embraced and kissed, begin to respond to the male's passion; they relax their limbs and begin emitting the coital fluid slowly and rhythmically.

Women of the Vana-vasa kingdom (east of Konkan) are moderately passionate; they can go through every kind of embrace and other forms of love-play that do not be come too violent. While they are careful to conceal their own physical defects, they take pleasure in taunting others with their imperfections. But they are neither fond of using vulgar and rude words nor do they like to have sexual intercourse with those who do so.

Women of Gauda (northern Bengal) are soft and sweet of speech, are responsive to the stimulus of caresses and have tender bodies. They are of moderate passion and, like the women of Vana-vasa, take delight in gentle love-play, hide their own physical imperfections and avoid both vulgar words and those who use them.

It has been said above that in order to get sexual response from man and woman the locally prevalent forms of love-play should be resorted to, since they are likely to be more expeditious. But Suvarnanabha observes that methods that are agreeable to the nature of a particular person are of more consequence than those peculiar to the locality. Where local forms clash with those that con form to the woman's tastes, one should adopt the latter.

Methods of love play, attitudes in coils and action during coitus that may be peculiar to one locality spread to other localities in course of time. It is, therefore al necessary to be conversant with the peculiarities of different localities."

Amorous cries, beating, biting, Scratching. kissing and embracing have the power to increase sexual desire in an ascending order, i.e., stroking is a better stimulator of passion than cries, biting is better than beating and so on. But they are complex in the reverse order; i.e., embracing is the simplest form of love play, kissing is more complicated than embracing, scratching is even more a complicated business than kissing and so on.

If a lover would not heed the female partner's warnings conveyed by gestures, words or expressions and forcibly makes marks or bruises on her person, she should not rest before she has avenged herself by dealing him a double number of marks or bruises with redoubled force.

Thus a SPOT or POINT should be returned with a SPOT-CHAIN, a SPOT-CHAIN with a BROKEN CLOUD, a BROKEN CLOUD with a BOAR'S BITE and so on, and she should at once act in such a way as if she were impelled by anger to join in a love quarrel with her lover. Having revenged herself in the matter of biting, she should take hold of the lover by the hair with one hand and, holding his face up by the chin with the other (i.e., tilting his head up), should kiss his lower lip in DRINKING-THE-LIP fashion. Then, wild with passion, she should shut her eyes and embrace him with her strength and scratch or bite his body in the same places as he had scratched or bitten hers. Embracing the chest of her lover with one arm and holding with her fingers the hair on the back of his head so as to prop his head up, she should hold him firmly by the chin with the other and execute a CORAL CHAIN on his neck. She may also execute such other marks as have been described. above. When even by day-time and in a place of public resort his own mistress would point out to him by making signs intelligible to him alone, and smilingly taunt him with, the marks made on his body by herself, the lover on his part should feign embarrassment at having to conceal from the eyes of the crowd these evidences of an amorous night. At this the woman, turning her head, will make faces at him and purse up her lips, as if in a vain effort to imprint a kiss and will exhibit to him the marks made by him on her own body with a show of great resentment in mock reply to his pretence to embarrassment, conveying to him that it was only right that since he had got the better of her, he should himself be got better of. This kind of play only increases mutual love. Those who engage in this mock love-fight and enjoy the game of mutual defeat in perfect amity will have unimpaired, vigorous love for a long, long time to come.

CHAPTER 17
ATTITUDES IN SEXUAL COMMUNION

WHEN both have thus become prepared for coitus, a woman with a narrow vagina (a doe), should, on the occasion of a tight-fit or extra tight-fit union, lie on her back and spread her thighs wide apart so as to stretch the vulva to the utmost. In a loose-fit or extra loose-fit union a woman with wide parts (a she-elephant) should lie with her thighs drawn close together so as to constrict her vulva as much as possible. But in an equal-fit union, where both the phallus and the vagina correspond in size, the women should stretch her thighs neither too wide apart nor too close together. These also explain what attitude a mare women will take. In normal circumstances, the hip is placed on the same level as the rest of the trunk, i.e., on the level of the bed. Lying in one of these positions: the woman will receive her man between her thighs In the case of a loose-fit or extra loose-fit union the woman may, to have her desire completely satisfied, make use an artificial apparatus, shaped like a phallus (dildo), of a size fitting the dimensions of the orifice or of a slightly bigger size.

TIGHT-FIT ATTITUDES

These attitudes are generally assumed by doe women in tight-fit unions.

When a woman, lying on her back, raises her hip with her legs drawn apart, the vagina is stretched and the orifice attains a great extension. Such an attitude is called the BLOSSOMING ATTITUDE (Utphullaka). Penetration is effected by the man placing a hand under the woman's hip and alternately thrusting in and withdrawing the phallus, gradually striking into the depths of the vaginal passage until the vagina has been lubricated by the discharge of the woman's fluid; or this may be effected by the woman moving her hips up and down.

This is important, for in a tight-fit union the sudden introduction of the phallus into a narrow canal may tear the frenulum (i.e. the strip of fore-skin attached to the base of the glans penis).

When a woman's legs are doubled up at the knees and the thighs are drawn upwards apart, the labia majora become separated from each other and the opening of the vulva forms the shape of an **0** (elliptical shape). This attitude is called the YAWNING ATTITUDE (Vijrimbhitaka).

When a woman's legs are doubled up at the knees and the thighs are drawn apart and so placed on the bed as to touch the sides of the body, the attitude so assumed is called the INDRANIKA (i.e., one that was recommended by the queen of the gods). This attitude, which is mastered by practice, gives so much extension to the vulva that even an extra tight-fit intercourse is enjoyed by the woman.

LOOSE-FIT ATTITUDES

In a loose-fit union, a woman should receive the insertion by compressing her vulva and the vaginal orifice drawing her thighs close or by squeezing them together after the penetration. When the thighs and legs of both the woman and the man are fully stretched on the bed, it is called the CLASPING ATTITUDE (sambutaka). In this attitude, the thighs should be drawn apart just a little to permit the introduction of the phallus. This, again, is practised in two positions, with the woman (i) lying on her back and (ii) lying on her side. These are practised in all countries,

If the woman closes her thighs tightly after the introduction of the phallus, it is called the PRESSED ATTITUDE (Piditaka). This will tend to dislodge the phallus out of the constricted vagina, but the man should try to keep it in place by means of forceful penial thrusts.

If in the CLASPING ATTITUDE a woman crosses one leg on the other, it is called the PINCER ATTITUDE (Veshtitaka).

This will tend to dislodge the phallus out of the constricted vagina, but the man should try to keep it in place by means of forceful penial thrusts.

If in the CLASPING ATTITUDE a woman crosses one leg on the other, it is called the PINCER ATTITUDE (Veshtitaka). This gives the maximum constriction to the vagina.

The woman may also, like a mare, constrict her vulva and hold the intromitting phallus so tightly that it cannot slip out on account of the compression of the woman's thighs. This is called the MARE'S HOLD (Vadavaka) and can be mastered by practice alone. This is practised mainly amongst women of the Andhra (northern part of the Madras Presidency) country.

These are the seven attitudes described by Vabhravya. However, the following further attitudes" are described Suvarnanabha:

When a woman with very large parts (a she-elephant) lies on her back and, closing both her thighs together, thrusts her legs vertically upwards and the man places his pelvis against the buttock of the woman to effect penetration, the attitude so formed is called the BENT ATTITUDE (Bhugnaka).

When a man holds a woman's thighs in a vertical position with his hands and brings her legs to rest on his shoulders, the attitude so taken is called the POUTING ATTITUDE (Jrimbhitaka).:

When a woman, lying in the above attitude, places her feet on the chest of a man and the latter holds the back of her neck with his hands, exerting pressure as if to touch her breasts with his chest and effects intromission, the resulting attitude is called the SUPER-PRESSIVE ATTITUDE (Utpiditaka).

If in the above attitude (super-pressive), one of her legs is stretched out, it is called the SEMI-SUPER-PRESSIVE ATTITUDE. It may be varied by stretching first the one and then the other leg.

If one leg is placed on the man's shoulder (as in Jrimbhitaka) and the other is stretched and Vice-Versa and the action is often repeated in the course of the union, it is called the SPLIT-BAMBOO ATTITUDE (Venudaritaka)

If one leg of a woman is stretched straight downwards and the other is flexed back straight above the trunk so that it touches the woman's head it is called the SPEAR TUIRUST ATTITUDE (Shulachitaka). This calls for high acrobatic proficiency.

If the man places on his pelvis the feet of the woman who has flexed her knees, it is called the CRAB-LIKE ATTITUDE (Karkataka).

If the woman holds both her thighs in a vertical position and crosses them so that the right thigh moves to the left side and vice versa, it is called the PRESSIVE ATTITUDE (Piditaka).

The woman lies on her back, raises her thighs upwards, flexes the knees and crosses one shank against the other horizontally so that a padmasana (a special attitude of sitting, resorted to by the Hindus in prayer) is formed in the air. This is called the LOTUS-POSTURE ATTITUDE (Padmasana).

If the woman, lying on her face, is embraced in the back by the man who introduces the averse attitude phallus from behind, it is called the AVERSE ATTITUDE (Paravrittaka). This is learnt only by practice.

All the above are attitudes to be assumed with either or both of the partners in a supine posture, lying on the back, face or side. These are the customary attitudes that are taken in sexual communion. There are other unusual attitudes that are sometimes adopted in coitus These are mentioned below.

UNUSUAL ATTITUDES

Suvarnanabha suggests that coitus in a lying, sitting or standing posture in water (of lakes, tanks, etc.) is a pleasant diversion. In the first posture, the head should remain above the water. either on the bank or on one of the steps. In the second, one should be seated on a stone step below the water-level, the third needing no particular base for the feet. Vatsyayana, however, is strongly opposed to this kind of union though it might be pleasant; for all these are countermanded by the authorities on Science of Conduct (i.e., prohibited by religious law). Such union has to be better expiated for by strict penance, Aquatic coitus, then, is wholly overruled and all UNUSUAL ATTITUDES (Chitrarata), as described below, are to be employed when both parties are on dry land.

When one of the partners, supporting his or her back against a wall or a pillar, takes hold of the other's body, while the latter encircles the former and engages in coitus, it is called the STANDING ATTITUDE (Sthitarata). There are three variant forms of this attitude. When the man raises up one leg of the woman and effects union of the organs, it is called the EXTENDED FRONT (Vyayata sammukha); when the man clutches the flexed knees of the standing female who places her feet on those of the man, it is called the TWO-STOREYED (Dvitala); and when the man takes the woman up by sup porting her thighs on the crook of his elbows, it is called the KNEE-ELBOW (Janu-kurpara) position. The last position calls for the exercise of great care. It is held to be approved by earlier preceptors in the Science of Sex.

When the man supports himself against a wall and the woman, holding her buttocks on his palms joined together, her arms twined firmly round his neck, and his hips encircled with her legs and her own hips moved by the kicking or pressing of her feet alternately against the wall or pillar on which the man is leaning, it is called the SUSPENDED ATTITUDE (Avalamitaka).

When the woman takes up the posture of a heifer, i.e., crawls on all fours and bends her head in the fashion of a cow being mated, and the man effects from the rear, also crawling on all fours in the fashion of a bull, it is called the BOVINE ATTITUDE. When this attitude is adopted, all that is normally to be done on the breasts (i.e., biting, scratching, etc.) will have to be executed on her back. In variation of this attitude in imitation of other animals at mating, coitus can be performed in the manner of dogs, deer, goats, asses, cats, tigers, elephants, hogs and horses. If there are other possible variants in the manner of other animals those also can be imitated.

When two women are wooed simultaneously, both of them loving the same man equally and persuaded to come to the same bed with him who performs coitus on both of them imsuccession, it is called the DOUBLE PERFORMANCE (Samghataka). If one man can do this in respect of several women in one and the same bed, it is called the COWHERD ACTION (Go-yuthika). When the man engages in sexual intercourse in water in the manner of male elephants in herd, it is called the WATER-SPORTING ACTION (Vari-kreeditaka).

In the Grama-nari principality (a small place on the north-western reaches of India) and Stri-Rajya (Women's Kingdom, where society was matriarchal single woman and women enjoyed the privileges which men enjoyed in other States; also on the north-western border of India) and in the Vahlika (Bactria) kingdom several young men are married and kept by each woman in her house, where they are enjoyed by their protectress either one after another, or at the same time. Those women are so inordinately passionate that they are not satisfied with the embraces of one man. The males in their keep, therefore simultaneously woo the women in such manner and by such methods as they can. While one young man holds her on his lap, another kisses her mouth and face, a third introduces his phallus, a fourth performs the task of sucking the mammilliæ, a fifth scratches the body so on. Each periodically relieves another of his duty and in this manner satisfies the desire of the woman.

The above also describes what is done when a courtesan is procured by several men and when a secret love is smuggled into the zenana of a king.

People of Dakshinatya (the Deccan) resort to coitus in ano with their women. This is a low form of sexual practice and its only claim to be regarded as a sexual union at all is that it is practised by a man upon a woman,.

Sexual union in which the woman takes the aggressive role will be dealt with in another chapter.

Concluding, Vatsyayana comments: "Observe the behaviour of those animals which possess the lower set of teeth and those that possess both sets, and of birds when they are mating, and adopt them to your requirements for wooing the object of your sexual desire. If women are courted with a perfect appreciation of their nature and the methods of love-play customary to their locality and in the manner of animals seeking to mate, they become very fond of, happy with and proud of, their lovers who take so much trouble to please them.

CHAPTER 18
STROKING, STRIKING & EROTIC ARTICULATION

STROKING and STRIKING (Prahanana) and the uttering of EROTIC ARTICULATIONS (Sheetkrita) are, strictly speaking, not parts of the process preliminary to sexual communion but are parts of the act of sexual intercourse itself. Vatsyayana remarks that there is an underlying conflict or opposition in sexual union, though it may sound paradoxical to say so. First, he observes, it resembles & quarrel, for both the man and the woman join to find satisfaction in their own different ways consequent upon the dissimilarity of their natures. Secondly, though love and sexual desire are delicate instincts by character, there is an element of violence in the sex act. A duality exists, therefore, in the sexual desire in both its instinctive and practical aspects.

Thus it is, comments Vatsyayana, that such ungentle activity as stroking--striking, if it becomes a little violent has come to find a place in the gamut of love-play.

The usual place where EROTIC STROKES are given are

(I)   the shoulders

(II)   the head

(III)   the space between breasts

(IV)   the back,

(V)   the buttock and

(VI)   the sides.

STROKES are administered with (a) the back of the palm,

(b) concave hollow of the palm, (c) the closed fist and

(d) extended palm and fingers (slap).

EROTIC ARTICULATIONS are the consequences of administration of the STROKES. They may be of many kinds. There is also another kind of articulation which does not result from stroking, but is due to the feeling of exaltation that sexual union raises gradually to crescendo. These are .called MURMURS (Viruta), and are of eight kinds, Among these are seven kinds of INTERJECTORY SOUNDS natural during coitus;

(1) resembling the nasal sound hing,

(2) resembling the rumbling sound hong,

(3) cooing,

(4) moaning or weeping,

(5) sound of forceful breathing,

(6 and 7) clicking sounds made with the tongue; and also

(8) other exclamations apparently denoting pain or expressive of prohibition, sufficiency, desire for being spared and also denoting excess of rapture, such as "Oh, mother!", "Let me alone", "Please don't", "Isn't this enough", "Let me go", etc. These really mean nothing but rapture.

One should often employ at frequent intervals, during coitus, calls of such birds as the pigeon, the cuckoo, the turtle dove, the cockatoo, the humming-bird, the snipe, the duck, the wild goose and the quail. Strokes should be administered with the closed fist on the back of a woman who is sitting on the lap of her lover.

She will, as if in resentment, hit back in a similar manner together with cries of hong, or will make the sounds of cooing and moaning, pretending that she has been hurt. When the introduction of the phallus has been effected in a woman she should be stroked with the back of the palm (Apahasthaka) on the hollow space between the breasts, slowly at first, and then proportionately to the increasing sexual excitement until the climax of pleasure in coitus has been reached by the woman. For there are three highly erogenous zones in a woman's body--the head, the hips, and the breasts. If these spots are properly stroked, even a woman who is slow to be roused to the intensity of passion attains an orgasm very soon and easily. Together with stroking a man should frequently and without any attempt at regularity of interval make interjectory sounds (mentioned above) in varying degrees of loudness (i.e., stroking with the back of the palm should be accompanied with interjectory sounds).

If the woman does not find the apahasthaka stroke congenial and communicates her dislike by expressions of displeasure or by protests, the lover should make low clicking sounds with the tongue (Phutkar) and, making a concave hollow of his palm, stroke her head with it. This is known as Prasritaka. This stroke should be given along with the cooing and clicking sounds made with the tongue and the mouth.

After the completion of the sexual act, one should give vent to heavy breathing sounds (i.e., should not restrain the heavy breathing that comes naturally due to profound nervous exhaustion incidental to ejaculation) and should also make moaning and weeping sounds (rudita).

A sharp sound produced by clicking the tongue against the palate which resembles that of the splitting of a bamboo is called Dutkrita.

A dull plopping sound similarly produced by clicking, which resembles that of a plum dropping into water, is called Phutkrita.

At all times, when the man desists after administering kisses, the woman should return them similarly and with erotic articulations.

When the man in a frenzy of sexual excitement starts to accelerate the strokes, the woman should utter those interjectory words as have been mentioned above, intermingled with moaning sounds, deep rumbling sounds. laboured breathing, low wails punctuated by groans and other kinds of murmuring sounds. And when she feels that the man is about to ejaculate the seminal fluid, she should slap him on the buttocks and in the chest with the flat of her palm and fingers (Samatalaka). If this is done vigorously enough, his seminal ejaculation will be postponed. This should be continued until the woman has achieved her own orgasm. While doing this, she should vigorously make cackling sounds like those of the quail and the goose.

Hardness of the body and mind and a certain aggressiveness and impetuosity, observes Vatsyayana, are natural to the male, so that his stroking is rather vigorous. Inability to strike due to weakness, fear of pain due to softness of limbs, aversion to striking and a certain lack of vigour are natural to women. This, however, is not invariably true, for exceptions are also to be found. Even a female may sometimes behave like a male on account of her intensity of excitement and excess of sexual vigour or customs prevalent in the locality. But she can keep this up for a little while, during which the male should act the passive role. As soon as she has spent up her vigour, the male should resume his aggressive role.

In addition to the four kinds of stroke as have been described above, the people of the Deccan (Dakshinatva) practise four other kinds of strokes. They strike their women's chests with the percussion of the clenched fist (kila), their heads with the extended fingers (karatari) and their cheeks with the fist closed with the tip of the thumb protruding between the fore-finger and the middle finger (viddha), and they a pinch the breasts and sides of women with a tweezer-like formation of the finger (sandamsika). This usage is so peculiar to the region that even if the strokes left marks or resulted in a permanent disfigurement, the woman would take pride in exhibiting them as marks a vigorous love! It is noticed that men in the Deccan beat their women on the chest with clenched fists.

Such painful and barbarous conduct, remarks Vatsyayana, is very reprehensible. These and other cruel and violent practices which may happen to be popular in particular localities should not be adopted by any one outside those areas. What ever forms of stroking may be employed, those that may lead to injury or pain should be scrupulously avoided Some instances are cited to show how violent stroking may lead to very unpleasant consequences. The king of the Chola kingdom in the Deccan, in an excess of sexual vigour, gave a courtesan named Chitrasena such a blow on the chest with the clenched fist that she was killed. Satavahana, son of Satakarna of the Kuntala kingdom, had altogether killed the great princess Malayavati with a blow of his stretched palm in the Spring Festival.

In this connection, however, Vatsyayana observes :

"In the matter of STROKING and STRIKING there is neither any premeditation nor any definite procedure according to the Shastras; once sexual intercourse has commenced, exuberance of passion alone controls all the acts of the parties. The behaviour of a couple enjoying a union and the various activities in which they spontaneously engage are of such a passionate character as to surpass even dreams. Just as a horse at full gallop fails to take notice of the bushes, pits and caves on its way on account of its blind speed, so do a loving pair become blind with the intensity of passion in coitus and set their minds wholly to the task before them, losing all sense of proportion and excess. Since one is liable to be carried away by passion during coitus it is all the more necessary that one should always strive to exercise one's judgment even at that time. Above all, such methods of love-play and stroking should be employed by one well versed in the science and art of love as would give the utmost satisfaction to both the parties to the act in consideration of the tenderness, weakness or strength of passion, and power of physical endurance of the other partner as well as one's own strength. It is true that one cannot employ all the methods on every woman with whom one has a union of on the same woman on all occasions. They are, how ever, to be employed at the proper time and in the proper place and on the proper person as far as possible."

CHAPTER 19
REVERSED NORMAL ATTITUDE AND TECHNIQUE OF INTROMISSION

WHEN during coitus a woman feels that her lover has become fatigued on account of long and vigorous movements of his hips and thighs without having lost tumescence of his membrum and without having his passion quenched by seminal ejaculation, she should with her lover's permission get him to assume a supine attitude(i.e., lie on his back) and should herself lie over him and assume the active role in coitus to assist her lover, by acting his part, to a successful conclusion. Of course, in certain cases the woman may assume this coital position because she achieves her orgasm more easily by this method, and in some other cases she may agree to do this to satisfy her lover's curiosity or her own desire for novelty.

There are two ways in which a woman can act the part of a man in coitus. The first is when during sexual intercourse (with the man in the superior position) the woman, in course of being raised by the man, sits up and gets on top of her lover by pushing him down on his back without, however, making him withdraw his membrum. the union of the organs remains intact, there will be no interruption of the pleasure that was being felt before and it will go on unbrokenly.

The other is to withdraw the membrum virile. Let the man lie flat on his back and begin coitus over again in the new attitude. The interruption in the communion involved in this method is justifiable only when the man has become physically totally exhausted without, however. losing his sexual vigour. In this case, the woman should. on account of the interruption, act her lover's part from the beginning. Having lain upon the man, the woman should loosen the flowers in her hair, punctuate her smiles with heavy breathing and press heavily upon his chest with her own breasts in order to get at his face with hers (for kissing, sucking and biting his lips and cheek). In fact, she should, in her turn, repeat all the amorous activities which the man had performed before. She will taunt him thus: "I was laid down by you and fatigued with the weight of your body. I shall now, therefore, make you as miserable as you made me earlier, by laying you down in return." She will threaten and chaff him in mock anger and return his strokes with interest, to take, as it were, a sweet revenge upon him. Now and then she will exhibit the shyness and bashfulness natural to her sex and will pretend to have become exhausted without having really become so. She will profess a desire to end the coitus though she may really desire strongly to carry the act to its natural conclusion. She will then carry on function in the manner of man, which is set forth below.

When the woman, lying on the bed, appears to have become sexually excited as a result of the amorous addresses of the lover, he should untie the girdle tied over her hips.

If she resists this, the lover should overwhelm her resistance by making her breathlessly excited with top kisses on her cheeks. If this should fail to rouse her to a passionate desire for sexual intercourse, and if at the same time the lover should find his own membrum in a state of tumescence, he should manipulate and caress her sides, thighs, breasts and other erogenous zones (q.v.). If the woman be bashful and if it be her first occasion of coitus with the lover, she will draw her thighs close together out of shyness. A virgin who is being initiated into the mysteries of the act of love for the first time will also close her thighs. In these cases the man should rub with his hand the space between her thighs, i.e., her pelvic rump and outer genitalia, with a kneading movement. If she is a very young girl or a virgin, she will probably cover her young breasts with her hands out of bashfulness and the lover should then rub her arm-pits, shoulders and neck. Such elaborate preparation is not required, of course, in the case of a woman who has herself approached a man for coitus. She will have to be approached in such manner as she best likes and as may be either possible or fitting under the circumstances. (For such a woman will have already been roused to a passion for the act.)

After this he should raise her face by taking firm hold of her forelocks with one hand and tilting up her chin with the other for the purpose of kissing her. It is quite natural for a virgin or for a young woman at her first sexual intercourse with the lover to feel very shy at this and to keep her eyes closed. But this should be overcome in the manner described above.

A man should look out for signs and hints of his beloved's inclinations with a view to giving her the highest pleasure in coitus. One of the ways of doing this has been well described by Suvarnanabha. During coitus, a woman will turn her eyes on one or another part of her body. The intelligent lover will make it a point to take this as a sign that she desires to be caressed in that part of her body to complete her sexual gratification. He will then press, squeeze, kiss, bite, scratch or stroke that part. Such treatment will bring her rapidly to a state of gratification. According to Suvarnanabha, this is secret with women.

The following are the signs of increasing passion in a woman:

Relaxation of the body, closing of the eyes, disappearance of shyness and reciprocation or active participation in the sexual act with growing willingness to unite the two organs as completely as possible. When this passion rises to a crescendo, she shakes her hands frequently, perspires, bites her lover, does not let him get up and withdraw his membrum virile from the union and kicks him with her feet. And after her male partner has had his emission, she puts herself upon him and continues to execute coital movements by thrusting her hips forward and backwards rhythmically. This can only happen when the woman has not been properly roused by love-play before sexual intercourse so as to achieve orgasm simultaneously with or a little before the man. This results in the failure of the woman to reach her satisfaction when the man has already exhausted himself by his ejaculation, In such a case, the man should, to bring her to the required state of preparedness, manipulate the inside of her vagina with the

the aid of his third and middle fingers extended together, which are roved slowly with a circular motion like the movement of an elephant's trunk. When he feels that the interior of the vagina has become soft and smooth to the touch, he should introduce the phallus. The vagina can resemble in touch (a) the soft ness of a lotus-petal or (b) the unevenness of a nodular surface or (c) the looseness of overhanging folds or (d) the roughness of a cow's tongue. A female organ of the first variety does not need this genital stimulation, for it naturally achieves early gratification. It is the other three varieties that are indicated for such treatment.

INTROMISSION can be effected in ten different ways as set forth below:

(1) The rational and proper manner of intromission or the DIRECT manner (UPASRIPTAKA) consists in the introduction of the phallus into the VULVA (vaginal orifice) and gradual, slow, deeper penetration with rhythmic thrusts and partial withdrawals.

(2) The phallus is held with the hand and moved inside the vagina with a rotary movement. This is call ed the CHURNING manner (Manthana).

(3) The woman's hips are lowered so that the vulva recedes and the phallus, introduced with a quick rushing movement like the infliction of a sting by a wasp, penetrates into the upper half of the vaginal canal. This is called the STINGING manner (Hula).

(4) The woman's hips are raised up so that the vulva protrudes and the membrum is plunged with a sudden rush up to its base. This is called the BEARING-DOWN manner (Avamardana).

(5) After the phallus has been introduced in its entire length, the man gives prolonged, forcible and jerky thrusts with it. This is called the PRESSIVE manner (Piditaka).

(6) After the phallus has been completely intromitted, it is repeatedly withdrawn up to the tip and vigorously thrust again into the vaginal passage. This is called the RAMMING manner (Nirghata).

(7) When one side of the vaginal wall is vigorously rubbed with the phallus after introduction, this is called the PORCINE manner (Varahaghata).

(8) When both sides of the vaginal wall are rubbed alternately it is called the BOVINE manner (Vrishaghata).

(9) The phallus is introduced fully, then withdrawn just a little; and, in that position, is moved up and down frequently along the vaginal wall till the conclusion of coitus. This manner is called the SPARROW-LIKE manner (Chatakavilasita).

(10) The member is introduced fully and as the concluding stage is reached by the man, the woman draws her thighs close together so as to contract the vaginal orifice. This is called the CUPPING manner (Samputaka).

The particular manner in which introduction is to be effected should be selected after considering the nature and strength of the woman concerned in the act. The vigour of coital movements must depend on the character of the woman's passion. When the man assumes the superior position in coitus (i.e., on top of the woman) the external activity (viz., undressing, manual stimulation of the vulva, etc.) will be different from that in coitus where the woman takes the part of the man (e.g., undressing of the male, stimulation of the membrum, etc.); but internal activity (e.g., intromission and friction) will be the same in both cases.

Just as there are ten different manners of coitus in the normal attitude, so are there three different manners in the reversed normal or woman Reversed Normal superior" attitude. These are set forth attitude below:

(1) The member being introduced, the woman "locks" the glans penis inside the vaginal canal by com pressing the labia majora. She also draws it in by a contractile movement of the muscles surrounding the vaginal canal and remains thus for a long time. This is called the PINCER manner (Sandamsa).

(2) After intromission the woman turns around like a wheel with the phallus as axis. This manner, called the WHEELING manner (Bharamaraka), requires much practice. In this manner the man should raise his pelvis upwards to facilitate the wheel-like motion of the woman.

3) While the woman is executing coital movements in the wheeling manner the man, who has raised the middle portion of his body including his buttocks, will swing it up and down and right and left. This is called the SWINGING manner (Prankholita).'

WHEN both are out of breath with the execution of coital movements the woman should place her on that of the man without disturbing the union of the organs, and rest themselves a while. If the woman alone should be tired, however, the man should lay her down on her back and resume the normal attitude.

Concluding, Vatsyayana observes: "Even if a woman conceals her intimate desires and tastes in the sexual embrace out of shyness, she inevitably betrays them out of exuberance of passion when she lies uppermost (i.e., in coitus in the reversed attitude). By placing his beloved in a superior position, an intelligent man should get him self acquainted with the character of her passion and her special tastes in sexual enjoyment through the style of coital activity she assumes (in this attitude). In this way he can gratify her sexual desire by conforming to her tastes on later occasions. A woman in her monthly courses, one who has lately been delivered of a child, a woman of small parts (a doe), a pregnant woman and a very tall woman should not be engaged to act the part of a man in coitus."

CHAPTER 20
CONDUCT BEFORE AND AFTER SEXUAL INTER COURSE: CATEGORIES OF PASSION AND LOVE QUARRELS

In this chapter Vatsyayana deals with some important matters relating to the behaviour of a man that have not been discussed previously.

The man of fashion will go into the house-garden in the company of his friends and attendants. The outer house set apart for pleasure should be decorated with flowers and perfumed with incense, and the bed, etc. should be properly made. Then the desired woman, who has bathed and dressed herself and has already taken a small quantity of wine should be induced by affectionate words to drink freely and take refreshments. He should then seat himself on her right side so that his right hand may hold the flask of wine and his left may be free to embrace her. He should at first rest his left hand on her hair, the skirt of her dress or her girdle. Then, to show his love he should hug her lightly with his left hand. He should engage her in witty and affectionate talk, as has been described earlier. Amusing conversation relating to various subjects, stories of an erotic character (or suggestive of things which would be considered vulgar in genteel society), should be introduced by hints. There should be vocal and instrumental music with or without dancing, and discussions about the fine arts should also be held. She should be. persuaded to drink again. When her behaviour shows signs of sexual excitement the friends and attendants present there should be dismissed with gifts of flowers, unguents and betel. Then, as the two are left alone in that secluded spot, the woman's pleasure should be heightened by the application of embraces, etc., as described previously, so that she wishes to take to the couch. This will be followed by the removal of the waist-cloth and the other preliminaries of sexual congress, as already described.

Such is the beginning of coitus.

On the conclusion of the act the lovers should, like two strangers, shyly and without looking at each other, go to wash themselves at two separate places and make themselves presentable, for the sight of an inflamed and disheveled partner may kill one's passion for the other. On re turning to the room after having tidied themselves, the lovers should seat themselves at a suitable place like two friends who are not at all shy of each other. The man should accept prepared betel from his beloved, on whose body he should smear with his own hand some pure sandal wood paste or other fragment unguents. He should embrace her with his left arm and, holding a flagon of wine in his right hand, should persuade her with loving words to drink out of it. Or he should persuade her to enjoy nourishing beverages confections or other delicacies.

Both should partake of such food as agrees with their tastes. Meat or rice broth clear soup, boiled meat, grilled meat with salads and sauces, ripe mangoes, dried meat and sliced lemon or orange with sugar should be eaten according to local custom and individual taste, on account of the invigorating quality of these foods. When taking these together, the man should taste of all the dishes first and present them to his beloved, recommending each dish as very sweet", "very soft" or "very pure and clean. If the lovers are inside a building, they should come out on the roof or on the portico to enjoy the moonlight. There they should carry on an agreeable conversation on pleasant subjects so that passion, satiated by recent gratification, may revive again on account of the refreshments and that renewed enjoyment may follow. While the woman lies on his lap, looking up at the moon, he should show her the different stars and constellations in the heaven, such as the Arundhati (the Morning Star), the Dhruva (the Polar Star) and the Saptarshi-mandal (the Plaw or the Great Bear).

In this connection it has been said: "At the beginning of sexual union as well as on its conclusion, love considerably increased by the use of refreshing drinks, perfumes, etc. When this is also accompanied by intimate and amorous conversation, a strong sexual passion is generated. If the lovers are both affectionate to each other and if each pay loving attention to the other ; if both pretend to be annoyed with each other for brief moments only and then eye each other lovingly; if they dance and croon songs of the amour of Gopa girls for Krishna (Hallisaka) or sing about the union of Krishna with Gopa girls (Rasa) as they are sung in the Lata kingdom, looking at the moon with eyes moist with the dew of passion; if they relate the feelings and desires that had arisen in their hearts at the first meeting and the pain they shall feel at parting again; and if, having done all these, they embrace and kiss each other in an access of love the sexual passion of young men and women greatly enhanced through the agency of the emotions the evoked."

As the preliminary and subsequent process (briefly stated in the present chapter, the former having been discussed at length in previous chapters) are integral parts of the complete act of sexual intercourse, it can be marked in three stages:

(a)   Introductory Or Prelude to coitus;

(b) culminating or waxing until it reaches the climax in ejaculation of the seminal fluid in the man and orgasm in the woman and

(c) remissive or "after glow" as described above. It can also be classified into seven varieties according to the NATURE of passion (Classification according to the degree and duration of passion has already been made).

These seven kinds of coitus are as follows:

(1) Coitus OF GENUINE PASSION (Ragavat)-This designates coitus resulting from a meeting arranged with difficulty through the help of intermediaries commissioned by both the lovers whose yearning for each other has been growing ever since they loved at first sight, or from a meeting of lovers after a prolonged sojourn abroad or from reconciliation after separation on account of a quarrel or a misunderstanding.

(2) COITUS OF INDUCED PASSION (Aharya-raga) This represents those cases where the lovers are attracted to each other without previous sexual excitement, while their love is still in its infancy; but it is fully roused and communicated from the one to the other through the exercise of preliminary love-play.

(3) COITUS OF ARTIFICIAL PASSION (Kritrima-raga) -When a man and a woman are really attached to per sons other than those whom they are copulating with and when the motive for coitus is not sexual attraction but the furtherance of one's interests, it is called "coitus of artificial passion". In these cases sexual excitement is evoked and heightened by the employment of the sixty-four accessory arts, such as the embrace, the kiss and so on, as far as possible, in the circumstances of the particular case.

(4) COITUS OF TRANSFERRED LOVE (Vyavan-raga)This represents, cases where the male, while engaging in the act, is thinking all the time of another woman, who is his real beloved. from the beginning of wooing to the end of the union.

(5) EUNUCH'S UNION (Pota-raga)-This name is applied to sexual intercourse with inferior female servants Or common whores or serving-women. In these cases love-play, such as embraces, kisses and manipulations need not be employed, for this union is resorted to for the relief of excess of libido and lasts till one has relieved his desire.

(6) DECEITFUL or CLANDESTINE UNION (Khala-raga) -This name is given to the union between a rustic and a courtesan, who takes care to keep stories of such union a secret. This union is generally resorted to by courtesans on account of excess of libido. Similarly, the union of beaux with rustic women like wives of farmers, female cowherds and wives of bird-catchers and scavengers and such other women, which is kept secret from others' knowledge, is called Clandestine union.

(7) UNION OF SPONTANEOUS LOVE (Ajantrita-raga) This name is given to unions in which both the parties are long attached to each other and have, from long sexual association, reached a perfect understanding of each other's nature, character and vigour and in which each assists the other in the technique of coitus according to their liking, so that efforts to adapt themselves to each other are not necessary. In this variety it is possible for the lovers to assume any attitude and use any form of love-play.

Just as lovers with a perfect understanding of each other's tastes and requirements practise coitus without restraint, so do they engage themselves in love-quarrels without risk. But in the average case, along with increase of her love a wife cannot tolerate the mention by her husband of the name of a co-wife who is her rival or any conversation relating to her or even being addressed by her name through mistake. Nor will she tolerate the transference of her husband's affection by his going to the apartments of a co-wife Should any of these be done by the husband, a great and violent quarrel arises and the woman cries, shakes her body in anger, tosses her hair about and tears it, beats her own head and face and strikes her lover, tumbles out of the bed or seat to the ground, tears off and scatters her garlands and other ornaments and throws herself down on the floor. When the wife behaves in this fashion the husband should, in a manner appropriate to the occasion attempt to appease her with conciliatory and endearing words or should fall at her feet without being annoyed with her, with the object of raising her up in his arms care fully and carrying her to the bed. The wife resists all his persuasions with angry words and recounts his offences again, resulting in a further increase of her wrath.

She catches hold of his hair and, pulling his head downwards, kicks him once, twice or thrice with her foot on his arms. chest, head or back. She then proceeds as far as the door of the room and, taking her seat angrily near the door begins to weep. Even if she is very angry, she does not go beyond the door lest her husband should suspect that she may be going away to a lover by simulating anger.

This, according to Dattaka, is a wrong move. The husband should go to her and by the use of various persuasive pleas try to mollify her. This will gradually please her though even then she may direct words of censure at her husband in order, as it were, to pain him. After a time she professes to be mollified and evinces eagerness for coitus and allows herself to be embraced.

Such love-quarrels are recommended, however, only for wives and widow-mistresses. In the case of a prostitute or a mistress in her own house, if there has been quarrel with the lover for the above-mentioned reasons, she will betake herself in an angry mood to where the over may be; she will show him how angry she is and leave him. Pithamardas, bitas and vidushakas commissioned by the lover will argue in his favour an will cajole her into being mollified. when they have persuaded her into an amiable frame of mind. she will accompany them back to the lover's residence, where she will spend the night. The lover. however, must not entreat, by going down on his knees, a prostitute or a mistress.

Thus a man of fashion can be successful in his object by employing the sixty-four arts described by Vabhravya and can enjoy beautiful and cultured women. Though many other branches of knowledge are discussed at assemblies of the learned, a person who is ignorant of these sixty four arts is not much esteemed in debates on the scope and nature of the three objectives of life. On the other hand, an adept in the Science and Art of Sex can, even if he is uninformed in other branches of knowledge, lead the discussion in assemblies of men and women. Learned persons, knaves — and even courtesans-all honour this exalted science. Who is there that does not give pride of place to it? When the preceptors selected names for this science in the Scriptures they called it Nandini (yielder of pleasure), Subhaga (beautiful), Siddha (successful), Subhagankarani (beautiful) and Naripriya (dear to women).

"A man adept in the sixty-four arts is regarded with great esteem and looked upon with love by his own wife and by wives of others, virgins and courtesans alike."

CHAPTER 21
THE DUTIES AND CONDUCT OF A SOLE WIFE HER BEHAVIOUR DURING THE HUSBAND'S ABSENCE

A GOOD sole wife should love her husband deeply, should act in conformity with his wishes and should regard him as if he were a god. With his consent she should take upon herself the care of his household. She should always keep the whole house very clean and so well-scrubbed as to be pleasing to the eye; she should arrange flowers of various kinds in different parts of it and should keep the floors and courtyard smooth and polished so as to give the house a neat and becoming appearance. She should make offerings to the deities every morning, noon and evening, and arrange for the regular worship of the deities in the family shrine. In the opinion of Gonardiya, there can be nothing more attractive to a family man than such a home. She should treat her parents-in-law, her superiors, husband's sisters and their husbands, the friends and servants of his household, with the proper amount of respect or authority due to each.

On a suitable plot of ground about the home (the kitchen garden), cleared of stones and pebbles, she should plant beds of green vegetables, plots of sugar-cane, jiraka (a seasoning), mustard, ajamoda, shatapushpa and tamala. In the garden attached to the home she should plant kuvivaka amalaka, mallika, kurantaka, navamallika, tagara, nandavarta and jopa trees and yet others that yield a large number of flowers and and should have plantations of of balaka and ushiraka prepared. Moreover, she should have beautiful seats and arbours constructed within the garden where wells and square and rectangular tanks should also be dug.

A wife should always avoid the company of professional beggar-women, Buddhist nuns, Jain nuns, secretly unchaste women, women magicians, women soothsayers and women who practise the occult arts of spell-binding, etc. As regards meals, she should have a perfect knowledge of what her husband likes and dislikes and she should also always consider what is good for his health and what is injurious so as to be able to select a suitable menu for him. When she hears the sound of his footsteps coming nearer or his voice outside the house she should at once come out into the outer hall, saying, "Can I be of any service?" and be ready to do whatever he may command her to. should dismiss the maid-servant and wash his feet herself.

She should not be visible to her husband in a secluded place without her ornaments and toilet on. If he is a spendthrift or is unwise in spending, she should reason with him on the matter in private.

She should attend wedding receptions, weddings, or ceremonial worships and, in the company of her female friends, social gatherings of her own set or temples of deities after obtaining the consent of her husband. She should participate in such sportive festivities as the "Night of All-waking" (kojagar-purnima) in such manner as her husband likes. She should go to bed after her husband and get up before him, and should not awaken him when he is asleep. I the daytime she should not rouse him from his siesta untill he has had his full quota of sleep.

The kitchen should be situated in a quiet and retired spot so as to be inaccessible to strangers, and should be well-lighted and always kept spotlessly clean.

If the husband is to blame in any matter, or in the event of any misconduct on his part, she may look just a little annoyed and displeased but should not use very unpleasant words. She should not use abusive language towards him but should rebuke him with conciliatory words when he is either alone or in the exclusive company of his bosom friends. She must never use any drugs or charms to make him love her. There is nothing that more completely destroys a husband's trust, says Gonardiya, than the use of such things. Lastly, she should avoid harsh speech, sulky looks, speaking aside to people, standing in the doorway or at the front door, looking at passers-by from the doorway, having private conversations with others in the house-garden and waiting or remaining in secluded places for a long time.

Perspiration, filth on the teeth and repugnant body odour cause disgust in the husband; therefore, she should always keep her body, her teeth, her hair and everything belonging to her tidy, sweet and clean. When the wife wants to meet her husband in private (in the drawing-room or the outhouse) her dress and decorations should consist of many ornaments various kinds of flowers, Sweet-smelling Unguents and brilliantly coloured apparel.

The proper dress visiting outing, etc., should be composed of two piece cloth of a moderate length-these should be fine and closely woven-a few ornaments, a little of perfume and unguents and white flowers.

A wife should emulate her husband in the observance of vows and fasts. She should dissuade the protesting husband by telling him, " Please do not press me not to do it." She should purchase, at appropriate times of the year and when they happen to be cheap, such useful articles as earthen utensils, cane baskets, wooden pots, iron pots, leather pots, etc., so as to be well stocked against rising markets. She should also hoard within the house secret supplies of rock salt and other salts, oils, perfumes, potful's of pepper and other articles which are always wanted, and also rare drugs and spices to provide against possible dearth and scarcity. She should collect and sow in the proper season seeds of radish, potato, swedes, spinach, damanaka (dona), gingelly, gonikarika, garlic, onion and other vegetables.

A wife should never divulge to a third person or a stranger the amount of her wealth nor the secrets that her husband has confided to her. She should attain eminence and excel all the women of her own social circle by her superior abilities, cleverness, knowledge of cooking, intelligence and deftness in other useful techniques. She should estimate the annual income correctly and spend accordingly. She should get ghee (boiled butter) from the surplus milk left over after the day's consumption, oil from mustard, jaggery and treacle from sugar-cane, yarn from cotton and cloth from yarn. She should procure hanging-nets for pots, ropes and plant-fibres (such as jute, rouselle etc.). She should supervise the pounding and cleaning of rice. She should know how to utilise the water and gruel of rice, its husk, its broken fragments and its powder as well as the charcoal from wood fuel. She should be well posted on the scale of salaries and other provisions for servants in relation to the time and locality. She should make arrangements for cultivation moving, planting and tilling and also for poultry and a breeding and conveyances. She should keep a watch the sheep, fowl, quails, talking birds, cuckoos, peacocks, monkeys, deer, etc., that may be reared in the grounds of the house In addition, she should keep an account of the daily income and expenditure. She should collect worn-out clothes cast off by her husband and, having dyed or washed them, should give them away as rewards or marks of favour to those who have been serving or have served her well or should make out of them wicks for lamps and covers for quilts or pillows. She should stock in a secret place jars of wines and spirits for use on appropriate occasions. All sales and purchases, including laying in of stocks and consumption of articles, should be well attended to. The friends of her husband should be welcomed with gifts of garlands of flowers, unguents and screws of betel (tambula) in the proper manner. The parents of the husband she should treat respectfully, always deferring to their wishes. She should not disagree with or contradict them, but should speak to them in soft, measured words; laughter in their presence should be mild. Those who are dear to them should be treated as dear to herself, while those whom they regard with disfavour should be similarly regarded by the wife. She should not be vain of opulence or too much taken up with enjoyments, and should have charity for servitors; but she should not make a gift to any one without the knowledge of her husband. She should so control her servants that they would mind their duties, but she should be liberal towards them on the occasions of holidays and festivals.

When the husband is away on a sojourn the wife should wear only those indispensable ornaments that a woman with a husband living must wear and should appease the deities (in the interests of the husband's welfare) by fasts and other customary acts of self-denial. While anxious to hear the latest news of the absent husband, she should, as before, supervise all the details of household work. At this time she should sleep with her mother-in-law and be guided by the advice of her superiors and make herself agreeable to them. She should setout with every care to realise all the money that the husband had planned to make and to complete the collection of all his partly realised dues. She should see to it that the current expenses are adequate and reasonable and all the transactions instituted by the husband before journey are successfully completed. In the absence of the husband on a sojourn she should never go on a to her father's place except on festive and funeral occasions. Even when she has to go on these occasions should go in her usual dress i.e., without pomp or grandeur) with her husband's relations or retinue and should return home in a short time. She should engage in fasts (i.e., should abstain from eating) on being permitted by her superiors (i.e., by the husband's parents or persons in loco parentis to the husband). She should augment the family coffers by holding sales and purchases according to the advice of honest and obedient employees and should economise on expenditure as far as possible. On the return of the husband from abroad she should first meet him in the weeds of a grass widow, so that he may know in what manner she has lived during his absence. For his well-being. she should, together with the other members of the house hold, worship the deities and make offerings to them.

In conclusion, it has been said: "A woman enjoying the sole love of a man, whether she be a legally married wife or a widow or a courtesan, should follow the canons of proper conduct that have, been described above. The reward of this devotion is religious merit, wealth, satisfaction of desire and the possession of a husband without a co-wife to share his love."

CHAPTER 22
DUTIES OF A WIFE WITH A CO-WIFE OR CO-WIVES; OF A WIDOW; OF A NEGLECTED WIFE; OF WOMEN IN ROYAL HAREMS; OF A HUSBAND OF MANY WIVES

The causes why a wife has to undergo the misfortune the presence of a co-wife or co-wives are: stupidity and contrariness: immoral proclivities: lack of attractive qualities such as beauty, health, animal spirits, etc., the husband's dislike to her: barrenness, continual birth of girl children only and the husband's lustfulness. A wife should therefore, from the very beginning avoid the misery of having a co-wife by endeavouring to hold the heart of her husband and by showing to him continually her devotion, her good temper and conduct, her efficiency and her wisdom. But if she proves to be barren on account of sterility, she should herself induce her husband to marry another wife.

If she has co-wives, she should strive to obtain ascendancy over them through the utmost exercise of her qualities. She should give a newly arrived co-wife a position superior to her own and treat her like her own younger sister. She should very carefully dress her rival for the night and in such a manner that the husband may get to know about her good offices but should not encourage the co-wife to become vain or impertinent. She should not draw the co-wife's attention to the defaults in her (co-wife's) duties towards him (so that the rival may earn his displeasure and her own position may thus be rehabilitated) but when she feels that the other realises her default she should affectionately give her the most useful advice (so as to remain in her good books).

She should teach her co-wife such arts as the latter has not been able to exhibit before the husband, taking care, however, to select a private place where the husband is within earshot. She should treat the rival's children as her own. She should be more sympathetic to the members of the household and more affectionate to the friends of the family than her rival, whose relations she should prefer more than her own.'

When there are many other wives besides herself, the eldest wife should associate with the one who is immediately next to her by marriage and age. She should cleverly instigate the co-wife who has recently enjoyed her husbands favour to quarrel with the present favourite. After this she should, to fan the quarrel, secretly sympathise with the present favourite and, having collected all other wives together, should get them to denounce the favourite as a scheming and wicked woman without, however, committing herself in any way, and remaining overtly neutral. If as a result of this, the favourite wife quarrels with the husband, the elder wife should take her side and give her false encouragement to make retorts and thus aggravate the quarrel. Should she find that the differences between the husband and his favourite wife are about to be composed she should herself do all she can to kindle it up again into a bigger quarrel But if, after all this, she realises that the husband still continues to love her rival she should then change her tactics and move energetically to bring them together.

A younger wife should look upon the elder wife as a mother. She should not give anything away even to her own relations without her knowledge nor should she use even the wealth given her by her people without the knowledge of her senior vis-a-vis. She should tell her everything about herself and regulate her duties according to the advice of the senior, and should even take the other's permission for going to sleep with her husband. She should not gossip about the senior co-wife with others and should show more affection to the others' children than to those of her own. She should obtain secretly more loving caresses from husband than are given to other co-wives and when her desire has been fulfilled by him should tell him that she

113

lives for him alone and on the bliss of his love. She that she should never boast to anyone of her husband's love for her or of his intimate caresses either out of a feeling of pride or from a grudge against rival wives, for a wife who discloses such secrets is despised by the husband. Junior co-wife, says Gonardiya, should obtain the regard of her husband always in secret out of fear of the elder co-wife's jealousy. If the latter is barren or unattractive and disliked by her husband, she should show sympathy with her and should persuade the husband to do the same (thus demonstrating to him the goodness of her nature and drawing him closer to her). Superseding the senior CO-Wife in this way she should monopolise the husband's affection and take into her own hands all the duties of a sole wife.

A widow who, unable to control her desire for sexual satisfaction and sick with the urgent demands of the flesh, takes to a qualified and pleasure-loving gentleman is called a Punarbhu.

According to the followers of Vabhravya, when a widow voluntarily leaves the protection of a "husband" upon realising that he is without the necessary qualities of a beau she may, to achieve satisfaction of her desire, have recourse to another person. Gonardiya is of opinion that as the cause of a widow's marrying again is her desire for happiness and full satisfaction, and as happiness and satisfaction are possible only in those cases where the lover possesses vigour of enjoyment as well as other excellent qualities, a qualified man with vigour is preferable to a merely vigorous man. Vatsyayana, however, is of opinion that what is important in this matter is that a widow may attach herself to any man who appeals to her tastes, the criterion for the selection of a consort being attraction, not qualities.

Two categories of "widows" are recognised in the Hindu code, viz.; (i) those who have not had sexual inter course before widowhood and (ii) those who have had it. A woman in the first category was treated as a maiden and could be married according to one of the usual forms. A woman in the second category needed no formal marriage and the fact of her having accepted, and been accepted by, a man was considered sufficient to raise her to the position of a kind of wife.

Such a widow should express her desire to be feted by her " husband " in such expensive affairs as drinking parties, garden parties, gifts to learned men and Brahmins and ceremonial presentation to his relatives and kinsmen: or in the alternative, she should fete his and her relations in the best manner that her means would permit. There can be no limits to the gifts that may be made her out of love (by the lover). If she is leaving the home of a dismissed lover of her own free will, she should return to him all his gifts except those made as a mark of love; but if she is being jilted, she should return nothing. She should take up her residence in the husband's" home as if she were a wife. She should treat his lawful wives affectionately, should be charitably disposed towards all members of the household, should conduct herself with good humour and easy wit before all friends and relations, should show her proficiency in the different arts and her wisdom in matters about which the husband is ignorant. Where the lover deserves to be reprimanded,' she should herself chide him. She should practise with the husband the sixty-four arts in private, should do good to her co-wives of her own initiative, should present their children with ornaments and should so conduct herself if she were their guardian. She should dress and decorate herself with flowers, ornaments, etc., with meticulous care and should make frequent gifts to the "husband's friends, relations and dependants. Finally she should carefully develop in herself the qualities necessary for leading social gatherings, drinking parties, garden parties and popular festivities. The neglected wife who is cursed with rival wives should take her refuge with that co-wife who most pleases the husband in a variety of ways. She should publicly exhibit her proficiency the sixty-four arts since it is not possible for her, on account of her bad luck, to show them to the husband in private (i.e., since she gets no opportunity to be intimate with him in private).). She should be a nurse unto the children of the husband born of his other wives!

She should win over his friends and through them should communicate her love to her husband. She should lead all other wives in the observance of religious rites, vows and fasts. She should be sympathetic to all members of the household and should never make much of herself.? In the matter of going to bed together she should, by conforming to the demands of her husband, though they may not be agreeable to her, bring back his desire for her company; she should not chide him with his want of love for her and should not show any repugnance to his advances. She should reconcile and bring round to a state of love any co-wife who may have quarrelled with the husband. She should arrange meetings between the husband and the woman he may be secretly hankering after and should keep the affair a secret. Altogether she should pursue her activities in such a manner that the husband may realise her devotion to and sincere love for him.

These conclude Vatsyayana's advice to wives and widows who form part of the household of citizens. The following observations describe the conduct of women in a king's household.

Supervisors of the king's household (Kanchuki: a Brahmin of advanced age and incorruptible character, and Mahattarika: an old woman of incorruptible character) will place garlands, perfumes and garments before the king, intimating that these have been offered by the honourable ladies of the king's zenana. The king will accept them and return them to the ladies as a mark of his pleasure.

In the afternoon, dressed in beautiful robes, he will inspect all his wives, all beautifully dressed and ornamented, together. He will converse with them wittily and engage ngly in a manner appropriate to the time, occasion, status and dignity of his respective wives. Then he will inspect his collection of widows and after that, his concubines (courtesans reserved for his pleasure) and the courtesans who dance, sing and act by royal command.

Each of these will have separate residences marked out in the order stated above.

The female wardens of each of the four divisions of the king's harem should. in the afternoon, when the king has risen from his midday sleep, submit to him the signet rings and unguents forwarded by the one among his women who is entitled to his company at night according to routine, by those who have been deprived of their routine rights and by those who have bathed themselves that day after monthly flow and should acquaint the king with their course. The king will decide his night's partner by accepting the offerings of one of the women, and his decision will be announced in the harem.

At the customary festivals and royal musical concerts women of the king's harem should be honoured with gifts of suitable clothes and ornaments and drinks. These women are forbidden to step out of the harem. Persons from outside are likewise forbidden to enter the harem unless, of course they are of proven good moral character. Behaviour of these Royal ladies with one another should not be such as to cause pain to others.

A man with several wives should look upon all of them with an equal regard and should not neglect any one of them. At the same time he should not connive at any offence committed by any one of them lest his forbearance may tempt her to do so again. He should not reveal to one wife the amorous play with, or the hidden physical defect of, another wife, or the names by which he and another wife had called each other during a love-quarrel. When one of them would complain to him about another, he should reprimand the accusing party. He should please one wife by courting her in private, another by admiring her in public, yet another by according honour and, in this manner, all his wives by different means. He should earn the love of the wife who is fond of garden parties by taking her out to them; of the one desiring sensuous pleasures by providing them for her; of the one fond of ornaments by the gift of them; of the one attached to her father's people by honouring the latter; and of the one fond of loving embraces by giving her loving embraces. A young lady who has mastered her jealousy and anger and who conducts herself strictly in accordance with the rules laid down here will enchant her husband and will gain a place above all her co-wives.

CHAPTER 23
CHARACTER OF MEN AND WOMEN: WHY LATTER REJECT LOVERS' ADVANCES: WOMEN FAVOURITES AND EASY PREYS

THE special reasons and circumstances that permit relations with others' wives have already been recounted. In this matter the following points have first to be considered:

(1) Whether the intended woman is likely to be brought round;

(2) Whether a liaison with her is safe;

(3) Whether she is within the category of forbidden women?;

(4) Whether it is, on the whole, profitable; and

(5) Whether one's yearning is powerful enough?. If the sight of another's wife kindles in a man the flame of sexual desire which waxes more and more in intensity, he may go in unto that woman only to save his life.

Such desire has ten successive stages, namely:

(i) the pleasure experienced through beholding a woman;

(ii) mental attachment; (iii) cogitation; (iv) sleeplessness;

(v) emaciation; (vi) distaste for any other subject;

(vii) want of shame ; (i.e., his overmastering passion can no longer be concealed); (viii) mental aberration;

(ix) swooning fits and, finally, (x) death.

In the opinion of earlier preceptors, the (a) disposition, (b) truthfulness, (C) chastity, (d) responsiveness to advances and (e) degree of intensity of passion of a woman are to be ascertained from a careful study of her physical form and the peculiar marks on her body.

Vatsyayana, however, observes that form and bodily marks are not unfailing guides to a woman's nature, character and habits and that these should, therefore, be inferred from one's behaviour, movements and gestures.

Concerning the natural inclinations of men and women, Gonikaputra says that women conceive a desire for all handsome and well-dressed men; likewise, men desire handsome and well dressed women. But due to various and reasons they do not mate together as soon as mutual desire is born. The peculiarity of women in this regard is that they do not care for propriety of impropriety in love and do not set about the conquest of me with an ulterior purpose. The reason for their restraint in giving full rein to their desires is the consideration that their private sins may become public or that their husbands may throw them out or that the men of their desire may reject and thus humiliate them. So when a man declares his passion before a woman and makes amorous advances and gestures, she may not respond though she may long for him by reason of her nature; nevertheless, she will yield after repeated efforts on the part of the man. But a man, even when full of amorous desire for a woman, is restrained by considerations of right and wrong and propriety of conduct; and one who is moved by such considerations will not succumb even to the open blandishments of a woman. Sometimes a man will make up to a woman without any serious purpose. Sometimes, again, having made partial approaches to one, he will not resume his overtures. Yet again, having made the conquest of a woman, he will become friendly with but sexually cold to her. It is often said and heard that one little values a woman who is easily gained but attaches great value to one who is hard to win.

The following are the reasons why a woman does not surrender herself to a man other than her husband:

(1) love for husband;

(2) consideration for her young children;

(3) advancing age, due to slowing down the sexual tempo;
(4) Sorrow due to bereavements etc.

(5) Absence of separation from her husband (so that the desire for mating with a lover cannot be strong or definite);
(6) anger on the suspicion that she is being approached out of condescension;

(7) doubt as to the real intention of the desired man

(8) fear that the desired man may be a bird of passage

(9) suspicion that he may be attached to some other woman;

(10) anxiety that he may not keep his liaison secret;

(11) the thought that the lover, being completely dependent upon the opinions of his friends, may await instructions even in these matters;

(12) fear that his overtures are not earnest enough;

(13) fear that a high-spirited husband may be cruel in vengeance;

(14) fear, on the part of a doe woman, that her lover may be intensely passionate and a horse male and, therefore, so vigorous as to make union painful (i.e., the fear of physical mal adjustment);

(15) shyness on the part of a lady to meet a lover who is an adept in the urban and amorous arts.

(16) the discovery that he does not understand the exigencies of time and place (i.e., is impatient and too importunate to be pleasant or safe);

(17) hesitation because he is already a friend of her husband;

(18) contempt because he is held in low esteem by people;

(19) contempt because he does not understand hints and signs;

(20) contempt on the part of a she-elephant female for a rabbit male;

(21) a feeling of compassion for the lover that he may not be injured through her;

(22) subsidence of passion on a consideration of her own physical defects, such as diseases, bad body odour, etc.;

(23) fear that her relatives would throw her out if the liaison becomes public;

(24) contempt because the man has white hair (i.e., looks prematurely old);

(25) doubt that the husband may be testing her integrity through this man; and

(26) conscientious scruples. One should at the outset try to overcome such grounds. for refusal by the desired lady as one may discover in her or in himself. For instance, the lady's love for her husband or her children, her advancing age, sorrow due to bereavements, conscientious scruples or such other reasons incidental to culture and civilisation should be overcome by increasing the keenness of her desire. The objections arising from want of opportunity or from physical disparity should be met by the employment of suitable means, such as devising an easy way of meeting together and the practice of the accessory sexual arts. Objections arising from the superiority of the lover to the lady should be met by intimate acquaintance and those arising from the lady's fear of his inferiority to her should be met by the exhibition of one's culture and intelligence. Unwillingness due to misgivings about the lover's disregard should be re moved by meek and humble behaviour with the lady, while those due to fear should be met by ample assurances.

Men with the following qualifications are often successful with women.

(1) An adept in the science of love-making;

(2) one who can tell stories cleverly;

(3) a childhood companion;

(4) a full-grown youth;

(5) an intimate playmate;

(6) an employer;

(7) one with whom there can be free exchange of words;

(8) one who performs pleasant tasks for women;

(9) an erstwhile messenger of a former lover;

(10) one who knows the secrets of a woman;

(11) a man who is sought after by superior ladies;

(12) one who is secretly attached to a woman's female friend;

(13) one known among ladies to be a lucky lover;

(14) one who has grown up together with a lady:

(15) a neighbour who is passionate by nature;

(16) a passionate attendant;

(17) a lover of the daughter of one's nurse;

(18) a new bridegroom in the family;

(19) a lover of theatricals;

(20) a lover of garden parties;

(21) one who spends liberally;

(22) one who is reputed among women as a vigorous bull man;

(23) a daring and courageous man;

(24) one who excels a lady's husband in intellect, beauty, merits and sexual vigour; and

(25) one who dresses and lives in expensive style.

Just as a man should know the qualifications for success with ladies, so should he know what sort of married women can be easily conquered. The following are the women who need little effort to be won over:

(1) One who stands at the front door of her house to stare at men;

(2) one who stares into the street from the roof;

(3) one who joins social parties of young men at her neighbour's;

(4) one who is always making eyes at strangers;

(5) one who looks around on being stared by strange men;

(6) one whose husband has married again without sufficient cause;

(7) one who abhors her husband.

(8) one who is abhorred by her husband;

(9) one who does forbidden things;

(10) a barren woman;

(11) one who always stays at her father's place (i.e., does not live with her husband);

(12) one whose children die frequently

(13) one who is addicted to attending parties in her own or her friend's house;

(14) one who strikes up familiarity with a man by her own efforts;

(15) an actor's or dancer's wife;

(16) a girl widow;

(17) a poor woman who accepts costly gifts from men;

(18) one whose husband has several younger brothers;

(19) the enormously vain wife of a mean man;

(20) a woman who is vain of her knowledge of arts and is anxious to consort with an adept in the arts as her husband is rather dull though not absolutely ignorant;

(21) one who is importuned by a lover to whom she was betrothed but somehow not married;

(22) a woman who matches her importunate lover in intelligence, character, brilliance and social position;

(23) one who by nature is attracted to a man;

(24) one who has been insulted by her husband for no fault of hers;

(25) one who has been humiliated by co-wives equal in status to her;

(26) one whose husband is habitually long absent;

(27) one with a very jealous husband;

(28) one with a husband of dirty habits;

(29) one with a cruel, impotent, lazy, timid, deformed, dwarfed, defective, invalid or old husband;

(30) a jeweller's wife;

(31) a rustic wife come to town; and

(32) one whose husband has a stinking body odour.

There are two slokas in this connection: "Desire springs from nature; it has to be nurtured by art. Anxiety and hesitation are to be allayed by the application of appropriate methods. Then will a mistress become sure of her success and steady in her liaison, and love will not be frustrated. The man who realises his capacity for success with a particular woman, understands the hints and signs by which she communicates her feelings and desires and takes appropriate measures to remove the possible grounds of refusal on the part of the desired woman, always succeeds in winning her.

CHAPTER 24
THE TECHNIQUE OF APPROACHING ANOTHER MAN'S WIFE

VIRGINS are more susceptible to personal approach than approach through female agents or intermediaries; but since married women conceal their passion they are better attainable through the efforts of female intermediaries than by personal approach. This is the opinion of earlier preceptors. But Vatsyayana is of the opinion that in all cases personal application, if it can be managed, is to be preferred and that female intermediaries should be engaged in those cases where direct approach is not practicable. Women who are venturing into adultery for the first time and who are on free speaking terms with the lovers are to be seduced by direct approach; other married women are often approached through female agents.

When the lover has to make the advances himself, he should at the very beginning become acquainted with the desired woman. Such acquaintance may be struck up either naturally (without effort) or through special efforts. They meet naturally when the meeting is held at or near one or the other's residence and they meet by special effort when it takes place at the house of a friend, a kinsman, a State official or a physician or at wedding, religious ceremonies (yajna), festivals, pastimes or garden parties. When he thus meets the woman desired, he should look at her with expressive movements of the eyes and the face, unloosen and tie again his hair, scratch his own body lightly and significantly, cause the ornaments on his person to jingle and press his lower lip with his fingers. Should the woman tarry look at him, he should talk with his friends indirectly on the subject of love and about his liberality and love of enjoyment. Or, lying or Sitting with his head on the lap of a friend, he should yawn and move his limbs, raise and lower one eyebrow, speak slowly, listen to her and, on the pretext of addressing a child or a third person, direct ambiguous words at her. He should make veiled appeals to her that may seemingly refer to something else but will easily reach the woman's ears, kiss and hug a child as a symbol of the woman, put betel (tambula) in its mouth with the help chin up and of his tongue and caress it by moving its chin up and down by the pressure of his forefinger. These should be done as opportunity and circumstances permit.

Then should the man fondle the child that may be in the lap of the woman, give it playthings and take them back from it. He should introduce conversation with her through his familiarity with the child and launch his business well by making himself agreeable to a person who is on fairly intimate speaking terms with her. He should make this an excuse to make frequent visits to her place, during which he should feign ignorance of her nearness and discuss with that friend the principles of love-conduct in a tone just loud enough to reach her ears.

When acquaintance has advanced further he should place in her custody things that would be realised after long and short periods and should withdraw a portion every day. He should also take from her perfumed things and betel-nuts on every festive occasion. To create faith in her he should give her a separate seat with his own wife or wives at his intimate family gatherings. To facilitate frequent meetings with her he should make personal efforts to accomplish with the help of persons obliged to him the business she may have with goldsmiths, jewellers, polishers, dyers in indigo and red colours and others: for, in the course of superintending the work of these people at her place, he will gain a long opportunity of seeing her openly. When having these works done, he should enquire if she wants other things also done, so that as the woman grows curious to know about those things, the materials required for them and the way they are made or constructed, he may show his own erudition by telling her about their various uses, their origin, their movement and transport, their costs, prices and availability and their practical application in a variety of ways. In discussing the lives of historical personages or the properties of different things, he should start a controversy between himself and her relations and, having set a wager, should select her to arbitrate on the issue (thus giving her an honour she will certainly appreciate). If the argument be held with her, he should praise her freely for being invariably correct (though she may or may not be really so). These are the methods of striking up an acquaintance with a married woman.

Now when a woman has intimated her mind by significant gestures and hints, she should be courted on the same principles as a virgin. But in the latter case the technique employed is subtle, for a virgin has never had previous sexual experience. In the case of a married woman, on the other hand, the technique employed should be broad and direct, for such a woman has had previous sexual experience and therefore, easily understands the appeal of the lover). When the woman has replied with gestures indicative of her acquiescence he should himself enjoy articles belonging to her and give his own things to her to enjoy. He should place on the woman's body his expensively perfumed wrapper and garlands and take from her finger her ring for wearing and also betel; and when he is going out to attend a social gathering or soirée, should beg of her favours in the shape of flowers from her hair. He should present her with rare perfumes desired by all. If these are sent through an intermediary, the receptacles they are sent in should be marked with nails in the manner of code appeals; if, however, these are handed over personally, the gifts should be accompanied by gestures and hints expressive of his mind. Thus, by increasing his efforts, he should remove her fears. Gradually he should induce her to go to a secluded place, and there should embrace and kiss her, put betel (tambula) to her lips with his lips and accept betel from her in the same manner. Finally, he should touch and rub with his hands the pudenda of the woman and so on.

One should not approach a second woman in a house where one is at the time making up to another woman; if there is an older woman in that house who has already had experience of adultery, one should bring her round with presents she likes, or she may frustrate the whole thing. If the man finds that the husband of the woman has been carrying on a liaison with a woman in the same house of assignation as his, he should not sleep with her mistress in that house even though she may be easily avail able there. An intelligent man having confidence in the soundness of his judgment should not even consider approaching a possible mistress who is afraid or suspicious of amours, is well guarded by armed attendants (like the wives of nobility), is worried by scruples and is possessed of a mother-in-law (who keeps a vigilant eye over the movements of her daughter-in-law).

CHAPTER 25
HOW TO ASCERTAIN THE DISPOSITION OF A WOMAN

WHEN making advances to a woman, a man should ascertain her reactions to his approaches; this is the way to determine the state of her passion. For a dignified and mild-natured woman will never clearly express her liking which should, therefore, be deduced from her conduct. If she does not give her consent though she accepts his overtures, he should try to win her over with the help of an intermediary. Should she reject the addresses of the lover and yet contact him again, he should understand that she has been in two minds and may gradually be won over. Should she, having once rejected him, meet him again this time dressed more attractively than before she should again be approached. If she meets him in a lonely place, the lover should know that she only needs a little force to yield to him.

Should a woman allow herself to be courted for a long time without, however, yielding herself to the lover, she is a cold woman liking the homage of lovers, she can be conquered by discontinuing the advances or appeals, for the human mind is nothing if not fickle.

Should a woman avoid the overtures of a lover and avoid meeting him at the same time without, however, expressly rejecting his advances out of self-respect and regard for the lover, it should be judged that she will yield only after hard and strenuous wooing or through an intermediary who shares her secrets.

A woman who rejects a lover's address with harsh words should not be approached again, but one who receives them harshly but later makes efforts to please him should be made love to again. A woman who tolerates the accidental or deliberate touch of the lover's body but pretends to be unaware of the touch is to be judged as in two minds and capable of conquest by constant and patient love-making. "If, while lying near her, the lover places his hand on her body or his legs on her legs under the pretence of being asleep; and if the woman pretends to be unaware of it as if she also were asleep, or pretending to be awake a little while later, removes his hand from her body to be sure as to whether he did this intentionally or unwittingly; if yet she betrays no coldness on the following day, she should be judged as desiring to have the same thing done to her again. If this goes on well, he Should proceed further to hug her under the pretence of being asleep. If he does not put up with the embrace and gets up and moves a way, but remains her usual self before him on the next day, she is to be considered as certainly desirous of receiving similar advances again; She remains invisible to him, she is to be judged attainable with the help of a go-between. If, however, she remains invisible to him for a long time but later meets him in her usual bland manner, she should be applied to with renewed efforts as a woman who has expressed by her action her acceptance of the previous efforts of her lover. So far about women who are reserved by nature and do not respond easily to the overtures of their lovers. There are other women, however, who respond who woman offers her respond more freely to these. Such a love woman is

(1)one who makes amorous gestures before she is approached;

(2)one who displays herself in undress in a private place;

(3) one who speaks in a tremulous voice and in inarticulate words (being in an access of sexual passion);

(4) one who perspires in the hands, feet and face;

(5) one who employs herself in massaging the head and thighs of the lover;

(6) one who, stung by desire, in the course of rubbing the lover's body mass ages it with one hand, makes her appeal to him by touching him significantly with the other and, as if amazed by the pleasure from the touch, embraces him;

(7) one who retains her hands on the thighs of the lover under the pretence of having fallen asleep;

(8) one who forehead on the thighs of the lover (in course of the mass places her aging) and when asked to massage his thigh-joint, does not refuse to do so and on the other hand, places one hand motionlessly there and does not hasten to remove it when the man chafes it between his thighs and

(9) one who, having thus encouraged the man to make forward advances, returns the very next day to massage him again.

A woman who neither becomes familiar with the lover nor avoids him and expresses her intentions by broad gestures in a secluded place without being approached, or by veiled gestures in the presence of others, is to be judged possible of conquest through an immediate attendant of hers; if she does not advance further after having made such gestures to the lover, she will certainly be won over by he efforts of a female intermediary who is in her secrets.

If however, she is not accessible after the efforts of the go-between, her case should be considered afresh before any further attempts are made.

In conclusion, it has been observed: " The first thing to do is to get known to the woman desired. Then come talks and with talks, mutual gestures and hints and responses in the same manner. Then should a man apply himself to the task of conquering a woman's virtue without fear. A woman who, at the very first meeting, comes forward to avow her desires by gestures, etc., should be quickly subjected to the processes of love-play. A woman who responds to the veiled addresses of a man by explicit gestures, etc., should also be judged to be impatient for a sexual congress and capable of being instantly possessed. The subtle methods that have been laid down above are meant for those who are slow to be aroused and re served by nature and, therefore, require examination as to their inclinations. But those women who respond with explicit gestures are as good as conquered."

CHAPTER 26
HOW A FEMALE MESSENGER SHOULD WORK ON ANOTHER'S WIFE

A FEMALE intermediary should be sent to contact that woman who has conveyed her liking for the lover by hints and gestures but is rarely to be met, or one who has made no response whatsoever.

This female messenger should in the beginning ingratiate herself into the confidence of the lady by posing as a respectable woman. Should she then engage the man's interest by showing her rolls of pictures embodying a story, instructing her in the methods of beautifying herself and narrating to her folk-tales, mythological stories and

and romances. She should then proceed to relate stories about the loves of married ladies for men other than their husbands and should further please her by repeatedly praising her (that woman's) beauty, proficiency in the arts, generosity and good nature. Then should the messenger gradually cause the lady to grow to dislike her husband by remarking, "How is it that an excellent lady like you has come to have an unworthy husband like this?" and, "Fair lady, your husband is not fit even to become your servant' and by describing with considerable exaggerations the secret defects and vices of the husband, such as the feebleness of his passion, his jealousy, unfaithfulness, ingratitude: parsimony, meanness of tastes, lasciviousness and so on. She should have an access into the secrets of the lady's mind by observing which of these defects and vices attributed to the husband disturb her. If, how ever, the lady is a doe by physical measurement, the fact of her husband being a rabbit by the same standard will not constitute a defect. Similarly, a bull or horse husband for a mare or she-elephant woman should not be considered to be a defect.

Regarding the employment of the female messenger, Gonikaputra is of the opinion that she should, after her loyalty has been ascertained, be sent to a lady who is making her first experiment in adultery or is making a vague response to the lover's appeal.

The female messenger should relate to the lady in details the excellent conduct in love, the agreeableness and the behaviour during the three stages of passion (i.e., the start, climax and remission of the coital urge) of her employer. If this should further please and interest the lady, she should then introduce, with the help of reasoning the business for which she was commissioned following manner: "Listen, O beautiful lady, what a strange happening! That so-and-so, a scion of a distinguished family, should have seen you at such-and-such place and become mad for you! He is gentle by nature and has never been so disturbed before on account of a woman as he has been now.

He is mortifying himself for you and it is not improbable that he may even die of disappointment." If the lady receives the news favourably, she should, on the following day, watch the words, face and looks of the lady to be sure that she is favour ably disposed and should broach the subject again. As the lady listens to her words with interest, she should narrate the stories of Shakuntala, Ahalya, Avimaraka, etc., and other current stories of happy liaison.

She should also describe to the lady the lover's youthful vigour, his expert knowledge of the sixty-four arts, his beauty, his qualities that make him desired by women and his enchanting manner of enjoying the company of women in secret, either truly or by inventing stories about it. While doing all these, the messenger should closely watch the lady's words, gestures and facial expression.

Should the lady concerned be favourably inclined, she will address the woman messenger with a sweet smile, request her to take her seat and ask her about her whereabouts, where she had been on the previous night, where she had had her meals, where she had been on business, how it had progressed and so on. She meets the messenger woman in lonely places, asks her to tell stories (about amours or about the lover), remains thoughtful, sighs heavily, yawns, makes presents of money to the woman, calls for her on occasions of religious ceremonies and festivals and dismisses her with requests to call again. She initiates talk about the lover by remarking to the messenger, "Well-spoken woman, what was that improper story you were telling me the other day?" She accuses the lover of faithlessness and lasciviousness and wants to get the messenger woman to tell her about the lover's previous attempts to approach her, how he had met her and how he had made verbal advances to her, without telling them herself. And when the messenger relates the yearnings of the lover she laughs, as if in derision, but actually says nothing of a discouraging nature.

When a lady has thus expressed her preference by signs and gestures, the messenger woman should increase it by reviving again and again the memories of the lover's previous attempts. And in the case of a lady who has not yet met her lover, she should describe at length the merits of the lover and, by the use of words that increase one's attraction, bring her round to a state of mind favourable for the attainment of the end. There is some difference of opinion among the professors in the Science of Love on this point. Auddalaki, for example, says that it is use less to employ a messenger woman in winning over a lady who is not known to the lover or one who has not respond ed with any gestures or signs. The followers of Vabhravya, however, hold that where an unacquainted lady or gentleman makes signs or gestures to the other at the very first meeting, there is certainly room for commissioning a female go-between. Gonikaputra is of opinion that where there is mutual acquaintance but neither gestures nor response a messenger may be employed. Vatsyayana finally recommends that even in cases where the parties are not acquainted and have not communicated with each other by gestures and hints, a female messenger may be employed for securing a union.

Having made the lady interested in the lover, the woman should now show unto her the enchanting presents sent her by the lover, such as betels (tambula), unguents, garlands, rings or apparel, all of which should be marked with his nails and teeth in a manner suggestive of sexual relationship,' the clothes particularly bearing manual imprints made with kumkum and suggestive of amour. should also show to the lady leaves cut in many designs, She representing different emotions and having love-letters inserted in them. The presents should include floral ornaments for the head and ears. Through all these should the lover express his mind. The messenger should induce the lady to send him gifts in return in a similar manner. When they are engaged in the free exchange of presents, the messenger should act as an intermediary for effecting a union of the lovers.

The followers of Vabhravya say that such meetings of lovers may take place during one's (the lady's) journey Suitable places to temples of deities, festivals in public and occasions for gardens, mass bathing ceremonies, wed secret unions dings, religious ceremonies (ajnas), entertainments and festivities, conflagrations, contusions due to scare about thieves, pleasure caravans, theatres and such other affairs that collect crowds of afford privacy. Gonikaputra says that union is easy of being effected at the residence of lady friends, female mendicants, nuns and female ascetics. Vatsyayana observes that if the avenues of entry and exit are well known and suitable measures are taken to provide against surprises and alarms, it is advisable to enter and leave herself, since this is always possible and easy of accomplishment.

There are eight categories of female messengers:

(1) THE PLENIPOTENTIARY (Nishishtartha)-She accomplishes her business by the exercise of her intelligence upon a full realisation of the desire and purpose of the gentleman and the lady. Her work generally covers those cases where the lover and the lady know, and have spoken to, each other. She may also work, on being commissioned ! by the lady, in cases where they know and have seen, but not spoken to each other. She may also move out of disinterested curiosity in those cases where the parties have no knowledge whatever of each other but where she thinks that the man and the lady are so suited to each other that their union would be a happy one.

(2) THE LIMITED-POWER MESSENGER (Parimitaviha) She is apprised of the measures already taken and the overtures already made and accomplishes the remaining part of the business so as to bring it to a successful end. Her scope comprises those cases where the lovers have already responded by gestures and signs but find it difficult to meet each other.

3. THE LETTER-BEARER (Patrahari)—She only carries messages, written or oral, from the one to the other Her task is limited to fixing up an assignation at a particular place and time between two lovers who are deeply in love and long for a union or have already had unions.

4. THE SELF-MESSENGER (Svayam-duti)--Commissioned to act for another lady, she goes in for the man her. self and becomes his mistress. Or she may apply her self to the man on her own account. She may act as if she did not know that her secret lover was the man to secure whom she was commissioned; or she may tell him how she had dreamt of having had a good time with him: or she may rebuke him with having called her by the name of his wife, with whom she should find fault; or she may exhibit jealousy of her; or she may hand over to him betels or other things marked with the nails or teeth and inform him that her father had decided to give her away in marriage to him; or finally, she may privately press him to decide which of the two-she or his wife—is the more beautiful. It is her business to meet the man at a lonely spot and secure him for herself. The woman who, having perceived the attachment of her object of love to another woman, goes to the latter in the guise of a female messenger sent by the man and having gathered news from her by fraud, goes again to the man on the pretext of telling it to him and then makes overtures to him, thus removing the other woman from his affections and substituting herself in the vacant place, is also a self-messenger.

This also describes the tactics of a male self-messenger who secures a lady by deception.

5. THE STUPID MESSENGER (Mudha-duti)—She is the simple-minded wife of the object of a lady's love. The lady wins the confidence of the wife, from whom she draws out information as to the sexual proclivities and efforts of the man, instructs her in the appropriate methods of satisfying him and dresses her with ornaments in such a manner that

the man can understand the lady's design. She will advise the wife to feign anger with him and will teach her to say to him words bearing a double meaning that only the man can understand. The lady will make marks on the wife's body with her own nails and teeth, conveying in this manner her appeal to the man. Such a wife, who thus unwittingly lends herself to the task of a messenger in adultery, is called a stupid messenger. The man, in his turn, will reply through his all-unsuspecting wife.

6. THE WIFE MESSENGER (Bharya-duti)—She is the unsuspecting wife, sent by her husband to the lady of his desire. He will cause the lady to confide in his wife, through whom he will convey his desires by hints and symbols and thus demonstrate his own cleverness. The lady will in her turn reply through the wife.

7. THE MUTE MESSENGER (Muka-duti)—She is a young female attendant who is innocent of all sense of guilt and is induced to go up to the lady's place by such unimpeachable means as gifts of playthings. When she has become well acquainted with the lady, the man should send to the lady, by the hands of the girl, garlands of flowers or ear-ornaments in which will be hidden love-letters or marks made with the nails and teeth. He should ask for her reply through the same agency.

8. THE CHANCE or WIND MESSENGER (Vata-duti)— She is a woman who has no connection with the business in hand nor has any idea of it but carries to the lady concerned a message relating to the current transactions between the lovers which is unintelligible to others or, on the face of it, bears a different or ambiguous meaning. The man should expect a reply from the lady through chance messenger."

Concluding it has been observed: "Widows, female soothsayers, female servants, women mendicants female artistes very soon gain the confidence of ladies and are well fitted to serve as messengers in love. They should cause ladies to dislike their husbands, should dilate on the

Attractive qualities of the clandestine lovers and should describe the unusual and highly pleasurable ways of sexual congress of which the lover should be represented as masterly practitioner. They should dwell at length on the passionate qualities of the lover and on the delightful manner in which he manages the business of sexual union and should report how he is sticking up resolutely for his beloved in the face of blandishments offered by many other women. They can, by the exercise of their skill in the use of persuasive argument, revive in the lady's mind projects she had abandoned in consideration of their inherent sinfulness or impropriety."

CHAPTER 27
HOW RULERS AND NOBLES ENJOY OTHERS' WIVES

FOR kings and their principal officers of State there is no access to the interior of others' homes; for since they are the guardians of their subjects morals and standards for their conduct, their own morals and conduct should be pure. This noble conduct is noticed in them and is customary. Ordinary people imitate them. All the world rises with the sun and watches him rise: and as he progresses in the sky, they set about their business. Kings and great men should not, therefore, depart from their traditional high conduct, for such departure is improper and reprehensible. If however, they should find it imperative or indispensable, they should follow the appropriate methods.

Peasant women-called "women tillers (charshani) by the Bitas-are available for the mere asking to the young master of the village, the young officer-in-charge of agriculture or the youthful son of the village patriarch.

" Sexual connection with these women may be had on those occasions when they are employed for unpaid domestic services, filling and emptying granaries and bar repair and decoration of manors, work in the fields, doing out cotton and the fibre of flax, hemp etc. (for making out in yarn) and taking back the yarn produced, purchase and sale and exchange of commodities and various other works.

Masters of the royal cattle in village areas can in a similar manner unite with female cowherds; and the controller of the royal yarns can likewise possess widows, lone women and vagrant women for the mere asking.

Thus the night police in towns, while patrolling the streets, can by surprising the ladies out for secret rendezvous with their clandestine lovers have sexual connection with them without difficulty: and officers looking after royal sales and purchases can also easily have their pleasure with women who come to buy and sell things.

On the occasions of the eighth night after full in the month of Agrahayana, the full moon night in month of Kartika (both being in autumn)and the night of the Spring Festival (moon night in the month of Chaitra) the beautiful ladies of metropolitan cities, towns to other urban areas often hold sports in the afternoon with ladies of the royal household within the royal Palace. On these occasions the visiting women hold drinking parties with the royal ladies, into whose separate apartments they go according to their respective acquaintance with the ladies. There they rest awhile in conversation and after having been properly honoured and feasted, leave the palace about dusk. At this time a female attendant of the king (or the feudal lord of the township, as the case may be) who has had previous acquaintance with the lady fancied by the king should, under instructions from the king, accost her and engage her attention by showing her the beauties of the palace and the gardens. Of course, she should have previously promised the lady to show her the beautiful things of the royal house on the occasion of these sports and, as the time arrives, she should do so. She should show to the lady, at the appointed time, the coral platform on the outer courtyard, the gem studded courtyard, the bower house, the vine bowers, the ocean-room (i.e., a sunken room cooled by streams of waters outside the walls, in which royalty retired in summer to escape from the heat), the hidden under-ground tunnels leading outside, works of art, pet animals, curious instruments and devices, pet birds, lions and tigers in cages, in short, all the interesting things that she had promised to show the lady. Now, when they are alone the woman should tell the lady how the king has fallen in love with her and should describe the king's cleverness in managing the sexual act. If the lady agrees to the proposal on receiving the assurance that the affair would be kept strictly secret, the attendant should lead her to the king. If, however, she rejects the offer the king should come himself, appease and please her with gifts and, having thus obtained her consent and enjoyed her to her pleasure, affectionately bid her farewell.

Or, the king, having bestowed the proper amount of favour on her husband, may in return have her daily brought to the royal apartments, where his female attendant will behave as in the earlier case.

Or, a lady of the royal household may, by sending her own attendant, get acquainted with the lady desired by the king. As their friendship grows she should, on one pretext or another, get her to come and meet her at the palace. When she is come, she should be warmly welcomed and provided with drinks of wine etc. and the king's female attendant should afterwards behave as described before. In the alternative, one of the king s wives may invite the lady of the king's desire to the palace, to the accompaniment of offerings, to see the lady on account of her reputation as an expert in the arts, and when she is come, the king's female attendant should act as described before.

Or, if the husband of the lady of the king's desire be either in trouble or in fear of trouble, a mendicant woman secretly sent by the king may approach the lady and tell her, "Such-and-such wife of the king gets him to do any thing she wants, and she lends a favourable ear to my requests and withal is kind-hearted, I can get you introduced to her in such-and-such manner. I will arrange for your entrance to the palace. And she shall save your husband from a great danger. Having thus persuaded the lady, she should take her twice or thrice to the wives' quarters in the palace, when the king's wife will reassure her. When the lady becomes exceedingly glad on account of the assurances of protection a female attendant of the king will act as stated before to secure her consent to lie with the king. The above-mentioned procedures applies to the cases of wives of seekers of jobs, those oppressed by exalted officers of the king or worried by powerful persons, those having weak cases in law courts, those wanting more money and power, those who seek the favour of the king or distinction at the hands of his representatives, those who are worried by their kinsmen or who want to be revenged upon their kinsmen or who want to bring others into the king's disfavour by making insinuations against them to the king and those who have other objects to serve at court.

In securing others' wives for his pleasure, a king should never set his foot on the doorsteps of a subject's house. In cases not covered by the methods mentioned above, he should get the lady of his desire to leave her husband's protection for that of a third person. And when she has thus attained the status of a public woman he should gradually take her into his harem. Or, having reduced a citizen's position through charges of treason etc., fomented by the activities of spies, the king may order the imprisonment of the citizen's womenfolk and in this manner introduce the lady desired into the royal palace. These are the secret methods of possessing a lady and are often resorted to by princes.

In illustration of the unwisdom of a king going to the abode of a citizen, it is cited that Abhira, king of Kotta (a small principality in Gujerat) was killed, when he was in the house of his mistress, by a dyer engaged by his brother. So was Jagatsena, king of Kashi (Benares), killed by his keeper of horses while conducting a liaison with his wife.

There are, however, customs in particular localities that permit kings openly to enjoy others' wives. In the Andhra country, for example, daughters of the king's subjects enter the king's household with a few presents on the tenth day after their marriage and are permitted to part after they have had sexual intercourse with the king.

In the Vatsagulma territory (a principality in the Deccan) it is customary for ladies in the households of the king's chief officers to attend upon the king at his palace by night. In the Vidarbha kingdom beautiful wives of the subjects are made to live in the king's harem for a month or a fortnight on the pretext of friendship with the royal ladies. In the Aparantaku kingdom (Konkan) the subjects make over their beautiful wives to the king or his chief officers as loving-gifts. And in the Saurashtra kingdom (southern Kathiawar) the ladies of the cities and the countryside as well enter the king's palace in groups and separately to sport with the king.

Concluding, Vatsyayana observes: "These and many other methods for the sexual enjoyment of others wives by kings are extant in many localities; but no king who is engaged in working for the good of the people should use them. That king who conquers his lust, wrath, greed, spiritual stupidity, vanity and envy conquers the world.

CHAPTER 28
THE WAYS OF ROYAL LADIES AND OF GUARDING WIVES FROM EVIL

LADIES in the houses of royalty and the nobility cannot mix much with unrelated males on account of being guarded, nor can they see much of their husbands on account of there being many wives to one husband. Their sexual urge remains unsatisfied. They therefore, obtain sexual satisfaction by the use of artificial means on one another. They dress up the daughters of their nurses or their female friends or attendants as males and fit them up with tubers, roots or fruits resembling the phallus in shape and with the help of these satisfy their urge. In addition, they sleep with persons resembling males in bodily form without, however, the characteristics of males. Kings, though they themselves do not feel any desire, may out of compassion for their lovesick wives, tie artificial membra to their loins and go in to several women in the course of the same night until the latter are satiated. In cases where, however, a king feels the sexual urge, or where he is due to sleep that night according to routine or where one of his ladies claims satisfaction on account of her monthly flow, he goes in unto those women of his own desire and gives them normal satisfaction. Such is the custom in the Eastern countries (Prachyadesha).

This also explains the cases of men who, being unable to procure normal satisfaction of their desires, relieve their urge by homosexual or bestial practice or by procuring artificial forms shaped like women or simply by masturbation.

Sometimes ladies in a king's household have lovers, disguised as women, smuggled into the inner apartments along with their maid-servants. In these cases it is the daughters of the ladies' nurses and other women employed in the inner apartments who make special efforts for arranging these clandestine meetings by explaining to the lovers that it is beneficial to them, that it is easy to get in and get out, and the household is vast (minimising the chances of detection), that the sentries are careless and the attendants in the apartments often absent (minimising the chances of being surprised during amours). But unless the ladies of the household have expressly desired it, no man must be let into the inner apartments, for that may lead to grave dangers.

However easily accessible a royal harem may be, says Vatsyayana, a citizen should not enter it for there are dangers abounding in that course of action. If, however, it leads to the fulfilment of certain ulterior objectives, or if he is repeatedly invited by the royal ladies, he may, after having made sure by an examination of the ways of entry and exit that the inner apartments possess several clear avenues of escape, that they are surrounded by extensive and deep pleasure-gardens, that they are divided into widely separated buildings, that they are guarded by careless sentinels and that the king is away on a sojourn, enter the royal zenana by the way recommended by the helpers. He may go in and come out every day, if he can manage it. He should strike up an intimacy with the sentinels outside the zenana on one pretext or another and should represent himself as in love with one of those female attendants of the ladies who know his real intentions, and should feign sorrow at not being able to win her. He should secure the services of those women who have a right of entry into the ladies' apartments to act as go-betweens and should keep a sharp look out for the king's secret watchers. Where there is no access for a go-between, he should take his position at a suitable spot where the lady of his desire, who has already given indications of her attraction for him, can see him.

If that spot be visited by the sentries, he should mention the name of a maid-servant as an excuse. When the lady looks at him again and again, he should appeal to her by making gestures and signs. In those places which the lady habitually visits (e.g., in particular spots of a particular garden or in a particular niche of the palace temple, music-hall, etc.) he should place pictures of herself, scrolls of lyrics with double meanings, playthings with significant erotic markings on them, floral wreaths and ornaments and rings. He should carefully examine the reply she gives(for directions as to a rendezvous) and then device a way of getting into the royal zenana He should conceal himself beforehand in a place where he is sure the lady will come; or he should disguise himself as one of the guards and enter the zenana at the hour when they are to be on duty there; or he should enter and get out, concealed in a roll of beddings and blankets or quits. Or he should not move in after having made himself invisible and placed himself within a chest. (The art of producing invisibility is called the Putaputa-yoga.) This is how that is to be achieved:

"Take the heart of a mongoose, choraka and tumbi fruits and the eye of a snake (or the Sarpakshi plant) and cook then in a sealed pot. This should be mixed with an equal quantity of khol. Applied to the eyes, this will make a person invisible."

Or he should smuggle himself inside disguising himself as a woman and forming part of the crowd of women bearing lamps on the Night of All Lights (the eighth night after full moon in the month of Agrahayana in late autumn). Or lastly, he should make use of secret underground passages.

In this connection it has been said: "The entry and exit of young men into and from king's palaces take place generally on the following occasions: when big and heavy things like wooden beams, or caravans of chariots and conveyances, enter or leave the ladies' quarters when a number of men have to enter them); drinking festivals (when ladies in come from outside); when royalty changes residence (may be seasonally); during the changing of guards; when royalty moves in train to garden parties or returns from them; and when the king has to absent himself from his palace for a long time (on account of an expedition, etc.). When a number of royal ladies within one palace know about one another's amours, they work in co-operation and persuade the rest to do like them. Thus when all the ladies have been robbed of their virtue, the whole zenana becomes determined to carry on with the pleasurable career of vice and the ladies, being indissolubly united, receive the pleasure of satisfaction early and often."

Thus end the observations regarding the secret amours of ladies in royal households. The following observations refer to the customs prevalent in several countries for an open pursuit of illicit sexual connections.

In the Aparantaka country, where the king's female apartments are not very strictly guarded, it is customary for the royal ladies to get well-qualified males to come inside. In the Abhira kingdom the ladies obtain their pleasure by uniting with the guards of the ladies apartments who are known as Kshatriyas. In the Vatsagulma territory the ladies bring in young citizens, disguised as women, along with women servitors. In the Vidarbha kingdom it is customary for the king's sons themselves to indulge in incestuous relationship with all royal ladies with the exception of their own mothers. In Stri-rajya royal ladies unite with kinsmen and cousins entitled to enter the ladies' quarters, but avoid others. In Gaudha, royal ladies have relations with Brahmins, relatives, servants, domestic servants and menials. In Sindhu-desha they unite with guards, artisans and such others as are permitted to enter the zenana freely. In the Himavat territory bold citizens enter the ladies' quarters by bribing the sentries. In Banga, Anga and Kalinga the Brahmins of the city go into the king's wives' quarters, in a manner known to him, to present flowers. They converse with the king's women behind a screen but even so they manage to have sexual connection with the ladies. In the Prachya kingdom nine or ten ladies together keep one vigorous young man hidden in their apartments and, having sported with him to their satisfaction, dismiss him. Thus is illicit love between women and men other than their husbands carried on. Now, just as a man can rob another's wife of her Virtue, it is possible that his own wife may be robbed of hers by yet another man. Therefore one should protect his wife from all these possible grounds of vitiation. Some authorities in this Science recommend that sentries who have been proved to be above the temptations of the flesh should be employed to guard the zenana. Gonikaputra, however, recommends the appointment of those sentries who are above the reach of both lust, fear and greed, for one who has overcome lust may yet allow others to go in from fear or greed. Gonardiya suggests that men who have been proved to be firm in their religious practice should be appointed, for such sentries will never permit any betrayal of their trust. Vatsyayana finally lays down that though such loyalty is part of religion, one does betray even religion out of fear; therefore, such sentries should be engaged as are both religious and free from fear.

The followers of Vabhravya maintain that a husband should cause his wife to be approached by female messengers, secretly instructed by himself, to speak to her as if from a different lover with the object of testing whether his wife is chaste or unchaste. Women are generally prone to yield to seduction, says Vatsyayana; one should not, therefore, set up such a test all of a sudden lest it should lead to the corruption of a lady who is yet innocent of vice.

Women go astray for the following causes:

1. Addiction to social parties of ladies, where there are much loose talk, drinking, etc.

2 . Absence of anybody to control her.

3. Immoral conduct of the husband.

4. Unrestricted association with males.

5. Prolonged absence of the husband in foreign parts.

6. Residence in a foreign land.

7. Physical privations (such as starvation, nudity, etc.).

8. Association with loose women.

9. Excessive jealousy on the part of the husband.

Concluding, Vatsyayana observes: "A husband who has become wise after studying the technique described in this section relating to illicit amours is never deceived by others in respect of his wife.

"The application of these methods only partially succeeds; failure is often met with moreover, it is sinful and extravagantly costly. One should never, therefore, run after others' wives. This section has been written with the object of securing the good of the people and the protection from evil wives. The instructions given herein should never be exploited for corrupting people. "

CHAPTER 29
THE WAYS OF A PROSTITUTE: HER HELPERS, TYPES OF PARAMOUR AND TECHNIQUE OF RECEPTION

EVER since creation prostitutes have derived pleasure as well as a living from sexual contact with males. Seeking men in obedience to an impulse for sexual intercourse is natural, but doing so out of a desire for earning money is artificial. A prostitute should stimulate natural passion even when her desire is artificial, for men put their trust in women who are naturally passionate. To show her love for her paramour, she should also pretend to be entirely free from greed (in other words, she should not make obvious demands for money so that the illusion of love may be kept up). She should always remain dressed in her ornaments, should keep a watch on the street before her house and should take her place in such a position as to be just visible but not too exposed to the public view. A public woman being like an article for sale, she should exhibit herself in a half-revealed manner to attract the interest of the beholders.

A prostitute should gather unto herself such helpers as are capable of attracting fashionable gentlemen to her, drawing them towards and keeping them away from other women, helping her earn money and protecting her from being harassed by paramours, Past or prospective. Officers of the town guard, men of the judiciary, astrologers, men of daring, strong men, co-pupils of the same teacher of the arts, disciples in the arts, itinerant professors of the arts (pithamardas), professional companions acting as procurers (Bitas), jesters (Vidushakas), florists, perfumers. wine-sellers, washermen, barbers and mendicants are qualified to act as helpers on account of their peculiar activities. These helpers should not, however, be allowed to become lovers.

The following categories of men are to be entertained for their money alone :

(1) An independent, wealthy and young man whose source of income is not secret;

(2) An officer in charge of a State department;

(3) one who has an easy income;

(4) a competitor in a prostitute's love;

(5) one who has an unfailing source of income;

(6) one who prides himself on being handsome;

(7) one who is given to vain boasting;

(8) a sexually impotent man who desires to be known as virile;

(9) one who is intent on outdoing another fashionable man in the matter of keeping a courtesan;

(10) one who is naturally a spendthrift;

11) one who is favourably listened to by kings and high officers of State;

(12) one who is extravagant from a belief in fate;

(13) one who does not care for money;

(14) one who disregards his superiors;

(15) one whose wealth is covetously desired by his near relations (i.e., a man without children);

(16) an only son of a wealthy man;

(17) a secretly lascivious ascetic;

(18) a man of daring and

(19) a physician.

For genuine love and a desire for distinction, a qualified beau may be entertained.

The following are the qualifications of such a woman's hero:

He should be of high birth learned in the science of logic, wise in the tenets of different religious faiths, an expert in the appreciation of the emotional effects of the fine arts, with lyrical abilities, an expert in writing and telling stories, an orator, a man of distinguished achievements, an adept in the different arts, respectful towards superiors and seniors in age, of high aspirations, highly enthusiastic, firmly devoted, full of forgiveness, liberal in spending, attached to his friends, fond of social gatherings and festivities on days sacred to deities and dramatic shows and drinking parties and popular sports, free from illness, perfect of physique, strong, not liable to drunkenness, virile, affectionate, able to guide women along the path of health and happiness and to protect them benevolently, affectionate but not too submissive to women, independent in earning his livelihood, kind and free from jealousy and unjust suspicions.

The following are the characteristics of the well-qualified belle:

She should be handsome, young, possessed of auspicious features, sweet-spoken, attracted by good qualities but not by mere wealth, fond of sexual relations with one who is loved, firm in determination, sincere in conduct, loving extraordinary objects, free from the vice of miserliness and fond of the pleasures of society and the fine arts.

The following qualities should be common to both men and women of excellence:

Common sense; a good disposition; propriety of con duct; straightforwardness; gratitude; farsightedness; unwillingness to enter into disputes; knowledge of right conduct at the right time and place; practice of urban manners and ways of living; freedom from penury: avoidance of excessive laughter and tendency to mischief-making and slander: freedom from fear, avarice, insolence and impatience; readiness to be the first to greet other cordially, and skill in the principles of sexual science(Kami-sutra) and the ancillary arts. All that are contrary to these are to be considered as defects.

The following types of men should never be admitted to sexual relationships by women.

One suffering from consumption or leprosy, one whose semen causes women to conceive and grow prematurely old; one with a foul smelling mouth (or alternatively, one who indiscriminately consorts with women). One who is too fond of his wife; one who is harsh mean or without compassion; one who is abandoned by his superiors; one who is a thief or a swindler: one who employs occult methods to gain his ends; one who cannot realise the difference between honour and humiliation, one who bows before an enemy for money, and lastly.. one who is too shy of entering into immoral relationships.

The following, according to the authorities, are the reasons why prostitutes give themselves up to men:

Genuine passion; fear of death or injury; gain of wealth; rivalry (one woman competing with another over the love of one man); revenge on an enemy (i.e.., a prostitutes gives up her body to an influential or powerful man to be revenged upon an enemy); curiosity (to find out if all that has been heard about the amorous qualities of a man is true); need of a supporter; exercise (a prostitute must keep herself in form for active participation in coitus with all types of clients, that with the intensely passionate type calling for physical stamina one is likely to lose without regular exercise); acquisition of religious merit (yielding to the embrace of an impecunious Brahmin, etc., was supposed to confer religious merit); reputation (this was to be the result of free promiscuous copulation on particular dates of the year); compassion (on a lover who may kill himself out of desperation); requests of friends (i.e., sleeping with a man at the request of a friend); shame; the likeness of a man's features to that of the beloved man, honour (at Having received the caresses of a great man): satisfaction of excess libido, a man's belonging to the same physical type as the woman; residence in the same house or neighbourhood with a client; constant company, and, quest of Power (being mistress of a man of power and influence).

Vatsyayana, however, is of the opinion that there can be only three reasons:

(1)earning of money,

(2) prevention of trouble, and

(3) love.

But a courtesan should never allow love to interfere with the earning of money, which is her main objective. On the question of freedom from troubles and worries, however, the relative importance of the situation should be carefully considered.

When an eligible lover presents himself and pays court to her, a courtesan should not at once accept his suit; for males do not esteem what is easily achieved. To ascertain the real character of the lover's attraction for her, she should secretly employ her cleverest attendants or masseurs, musicians, and jesters or persons devoted to the lover, to be near him (and find out whether it is a passing fancy or a genuine passion on his part). In the absence of these, she should employ a Pithamarda (an itinerant tutor of fashionable behaviour). From them she should learn about the purity or baseness of his technique of love making (whether he is fond of normal or perverse methods and so on), the type and character of his passion and his tastes in women, the quality of his attachment (whether his attachment is likely to be temporary or permanent etc.) and his liberality or parsimony. Having made herself sure that the lover means genuine business, she should get into intimate acquaintance with him through the agency of a Bita'. This should be brought about by getting a Pithamarda to bring the lover to the courtesan's residence on the pretext of witnessing a fight between quails, cocks or rams or a talking duel between pet birds or theatricals or a musical concert: conversely, the prostitute may get herself invited to the lover's place. On the arrival of the lover to her place she should entertain him and put him in excellent humour and should present him, as a love gift with some thing or other, exhorting him to use it personally. She should please him by holding social gatherings of the kind which the lover particularly likes and by appropriate means for showing him honour (i.e. by presenting rare perfumes, garlands, etc., such as are presented to very distinguished guests). Then, when the man has departed from her place, she should frequently send presents to him by the hands of a female attendant who can talk well and wittily. She should also sometimes personally go to the man's residence, accompanied by a Pithamarda, on one pretext or another.

In this matter, there are the following slokas:

"When the paramour-to-be presents himself at prostitute's place, she should receive him lovingly with presents of betel, garlands and fine unguents and should arrange music and dance recitals and social gatherings. When he has become enamoured of her, gifts should be given and rings and wraps exchanged. Suggestive hints about sexual intercourse should be thrown by her own people (i.e., she should not make the suggestion herself, for forward behaviour makes women cheap in the eyes of men), or through loving-gifts (the absolute character of these gifts will make the infatuated paramour think that she is prepared to give up everything to her) or through invitations from Pithamardas or other attendants to spend the night there or by the application of the technique of sexual approach (such as reciprocating energetically to his embrace, kisses, etc.). Having in this manner got him to lie with her, she should later intimate him more and more into the pleasures of love."

CHAPTER 30
HOW A PROSTITUTE SHOULD PLEASE HER PARAMOUR BY ADOPTING WAYS OF A WIFE

HAVING secured the paramour, the prostitute, to please him, should act like a devoted and sole wife. She should make him more and more infatuated without falling in love with him herself; but she should pretend as if she had become attached to him: this, in brief, is what is to be done. She should be under the control of her mother, who will act the part of a cruel and covetous woman. If she has no mother, she should fake up one. This mother should behave as if she were not much pleased with the paramour and should sometimes forcibly take the woman away from his company (as if to compel her daughter to transfer her attentions to another paramour: this pretence sometimes yields a lot of money from an infatuated paramour). At this the prostitute should feign bashfulness, fear and want of interest in, and disgust with, every thing; all the same, she should not disobey her mother's" orders. She should inform the paramour that she has been suffering from an imaginary illness that is not loathsome, is sudden and irregular in its onset and is not apparent to the eye (e.g., headache, migraine, etc.), so that she may put this up as an excuse for not having come into him, whatever the real reason for the avoidance. Nevertheless, she should send her maid-servant to him for a few flowers and garlands used by him and a few of his betels.

When the paramour has sexual intercourse with her, the prostitute should express wonder at the artistry of his approach and should display her willingness to learn from him the sixty-four techniques of approach. She should persuade the paramour himself to give repeated demonstrations of the lessons he gives in the technique of approach. She should privately practise the arts that give him particular pleasure and should confide to him the most intimate desires. She should take care to keep concealed whatever defects there may be in the private parts of her body. When the paramour turns round in bed she should so lie as to face him and should return his gaze lovingly. She should acquiesce when he caresses her pudenda and should kiss and embrace him when he is asleep.

When he is absent-minded, she should look at him anxiously (as if in concern for his trouble or worry) When he is in the street, she should watch him from her house and should he chance to see her at it, she should feign shyness (as if her secret love for him had been betrayed); this is the way to disarm all his possible suspicions of her inconstancy. She should profess to abhor all that he dislikes and love all that he likes, praise the excellence of all he thinks attractive and express joy in his happiness and sorrow in his sorrow.

She should set up enquiries as to whether he is attached to any other female (a demonstration of amorous jealousy); should feign short spells of displeasure with him and should profess her concern by imputing to some other women the tooth-and-nail marks she herself had previously made on him. She should not express her desire for a sexual congress by words, signs or gestures. She may, however, express that desire in words by pretending to be talking in her sleep under the stress of illness, if she finds her hints unavailing.

A prostitute should make frequent mention of the meritorious deeds of her beau. She should understand the real implications of the words he says and having ascertained them, should refer to them with praise. She should follow up his lead in talk to show him her wisdom and learning. When she has won his love she should express as a rule her agreement with all his views except on the matter of his wife or wives. Whenever the beau sighs. yawns. slips. Stumbles or falls, she should express her concern as if in anxiety for his welfare; whenever he sneezes, has a fit of coughing in the midst of conversation or shows amazement, she should say, to show her affection, "May you live to be a hundred or a thousand." Whenever he may be in a melancholy mood, she should enquire whether it is due to illness or to hostility of anybody. She should not praise a third person in his presence nor should she criticise any person for a defect that may equally be shared by her beau. She should wear the gifts of her lover, however insignificant they may be. If false accusations are made against the paramour or if a sorrow such as a bereavement or an illness befalls him, she should pull off her ornaments, feign aversion to food, bemoan the trouble, profess her determination to leave the kingdom with him and even offer to buy him out of his debts and obligations to the king. She should say that, having got him, she has achieved her life's highest bliss. Should the lover gain wealth or succeed in a particular objective or regain his health she should fulfil her vows, announced previously, to the gods and take up her ornaments again for constant wear. But she should take care not to eat too much. She should mention in her songs the personal name and clan name of the lover. She should feign a headache and (after laying herself down the bed), having taken the lover's hand in her own, should place it on her head and brow and feign to fall asleep at its soothing touch; or she should recline on his lap and feign sleep. Should he go away for a short time, she should go with him, saying that she cannot brook even the briefest separation from him. She should profess a desire to have a son by him and to precede him in death.

A prostitute should not converse in private with anybody in a manner unknown to her lover. She should dissuade him from undertaking vows simulates the and fasts by maintaining that the sin of non-observance of these may be visited on her; and if her persuasions are not successful she should herself undertake them along with him. Should there be an argument with any person over any matter, she should mention her lover and point out how impossible it would be for the arguer to establish the point since it would even be impossible for her lover himself. She should regard the people of her lover and her own people with equal esteem. She should join no soirée without her lover's company, should profess honour at being able to wear his left-over garlands etc. and partake of the remnants of his dishes and should praise the lineage, culture, learning, caste, colour, riches, native place, wealth of friends, qualities, youth and affability of her lover. She should have connoisseurs and experts sent to the place where the lover may have arranged a concert, should follow him wherever he may go without fearing the rigours of winter, summer or rains and, while performing a religious rite, should express a desire to be united with the lover in the next birth. She should adopt the technique of amour, the coital activity and the passional behaviour that are pleasing to the lover, should express anxiety lest others should bewitch him out of his love for her and, to demonstrate her love for him, should always quarrel with her mother (real or so-called) over the question of going out to the over (and refusing the advances of other clients). If this mother leads her forcibly (all faked) to another keeper, she should threaten (but not actually attempt) suicide by poison, fasting, stabbing or hanging and, by informing the lover of her resolve through a messenger, should have his confidence in her lovalty restored. Or she should curse her own profession that compels her to renounce love at her mother's commands or for filthy lucre. Nevertheless she should not dispute with her mother over the question of money and, in fact, should do nothing without her mother's advice.

When the lover sets out for foreign parts, a prostitute should extract an oath from him that he would return soon and, so long as he is away she should retrain rom toilet and wearing of all ornaments and decorations except only bangles made of conch-shells (such as wives wear as a charm for the welfare of their husbands) in of his welfare. She should allude to reminiscences of the days enjoyed with the lover, should visit female sooth-sayers and occultists who speak about the future from divine inspiration and should profess a desire to be in the position of the stars, the moon and the sun so that she could see the lover and he could see her in his distant sojourn. She should describe in details to people attached to the lover happy dreams about him that she had during the preceding night and express her longing for his safe and early return; should she have dreamt bad dreams, she should profess concern and have sacred rites performed to pacify the agents of evil. When the lover returns she should offer worship to the God of Love (Kamadeva), make votive offerings to all the gods, have cloths bought in by her female companions for distribution and make offering of lumps of food to crows, saying that she had promised to do all these if the lover came safe to her. All these except the feeding of the crows should be done also Subsequent to the first visit of the lover to her (i.e.., when the prostitute first passed into his keeping).

She should keep on telling that she would have followed her lover. so deeply attached to her, in death if he had died (away from home).

The following are the characteristics of one who is deeply attached:

One who places complete reliance on the professions and opinions of a woman, has the same tastes and inclinations as the woman in matters of sexual union, fulfils her desires whatever their nature, is afraid of nothing for her love (i.e., cares nothing for scandal, impropriety or social punishment) and has no thought for himself in his attachment to her is called a deeply attached person.

The above have been extracted from the treatise composed by Dattaka as an illustration. What has been left unsaid should be gathered from men experienced in these matters and from an examination of the nature of males.

There are two aphorisms? in this connection:

"Even experts can hardly ascertain from signs and gestures whether a prostitute's love is genuine or assumed. For very thin is the line between genuine and simulated passion, there being no material standards of judgment as to passion; women can simulate out of abounding greed all the outward behaviour incidental to genuine attachment; and as for men, they are indiscriminating by nature, trust women who profess love for them and act in obedience to the sexual impulse. Prostitutes are passionately in love at one moment and absolutely cold at the next; they take pains to please at one moment and abandon their lovers at the next after having extracted all their wealth. It is impossible, therefore, to understand the ways of prostitutes."

CHAPTER 31
HOW A COURTESAN EARNS MONEY AND HOW SHE EXPELS THE IMPOVERISHED LOVER

THERE are two ways of extracting wealth out of deeply attached paramours:

(1) the natural, i.e., easy way and

(2) the methodical, i.e., carefully planned way.

Some preceptors are of the opinion that if a prostitute receives more wealth than was expected by her without any effort on her part she should not exert herself to get still more wealth. Vatsyayana, however, is of the opinion that even where the requisite income without effort is assured, the paramour will part twice as much if suitable methods are followed.

The following are some of the ways in which a prostitute can extract money from her paramour without causing an impression of avarice:

When dealers in ornaments, sweetmeats, condiments specially prepared dishes, beverages, garlands, cloths, perfumes or other articles call at her place, she should, in the presence of the paramour, purchase their wares by paying for them on the spot, though the accounts could have been settled later in the usual course of business so that her eagerness to have the things may cause the paramour to pay for it. She should praise valuable articles belonging to them in his presence so that he may think she has a great desire for them and may present her with them. She should tell him about her impending celebration of a Sacred vow or a tree-planting ceremony or the founding of a public rest-house within a garden, or the establishment of shrine or excavation of a public water-reservoir or garden festivities and should make the necessity of making love gifts to the invited guests at these ceremonies a convenient excuse for taking money from him. She should report to him that while coming out to him at night, town guards or burglars, as the case may be, of course by previous arrangement with them-had detained her and robbed her of her ornaments, so that the paramour, thinking that she had lost her ornaments coming to him out of love may pay for a new set. She should also report the loss of her property by fire or theft or through the carelessness of her mother and should include in the alleged loss not only her own valuables but ornaments represented as borrowed from others for wearing on a special occasion (e.g., a party) as also ornaments given her by the paramour. She should bring to his ears through à secret agent of hers (who passes as a friend of his reports of costs incurred by her in arranging nightly visits to his place. She should contract debts (by arrangement) to defray expenses connected with the paramour's parties and fake up a quarrel over this with her mother in his presence. She should cleverly get him to know of her in ability to attend a ceremony at the house of a friend on account of her inability, through having no money, to manage suitable presents; she should, of course, have in formed him beforehand that this particular friend had on a previous occasion given her valuable presents. She should make cuts in the expense that are indispensable for maintenance of her health in such a manner that he gets to know about it. She should commission artistes on behalf of the paramour (she would go shares with the artistes over the latter's profits). She should perform good offices to physicians and high State officers on convenient occasions so that they may, when required, extort money out of the paramour. She should help the friends and well-wishers of the paramour in their troubles so that they may in their turn be inclined to persuade him to pay her more money. She should get him to pay for repairs to her residence and to contribute liberally to the alleged expenses of the sacred ceremonies (like the first rice ceremony, the first hair-cutting ceremony, etc.) of a female friend's son or of the fulfilment of the friend's yearnings or of her medical treatment or even of relieving her of her distress. She should sell one or two of her ornaments for the sake of the paramour in his very presence so as to compel him to find more money for her. She should negotiate with dealers (having previously made arrangements with them regarding the false transactions for the "sale" of ornaments, furniture and utensils dear to her so that the paramour may think she must be very short of money to be compelled to dispose of her daily necessaries and may give her more money. She should, on the pretext that her chattels have been mixed up with and exchanged for, those of a neighbouring courtesan on account of their similarity, purchase a new set of superior utensils.

A prostitute should constantly recall and recite the past munificence of her paramour, should get secret agents to tell him how her neighbouring courtesan have been earning more than she and in his presence, should herself describe before them (the neighbours) with every appearance of reluctance, whether her story is true or made up, how she is being lavishly paid. She should circulate stories to the effect that she would publicly reject, or that she has been rejecting the offers made by discarded former paramours for a resumption of relationships by promising lager payments. These stories will so please him that he will gladly pay more. She should bring to his attention how beaux who wanted to compete with him in fashionable behaviour have been spending more generously. Or she should have a boy sent to the paramour at his residence (when he is carousing in the company of friends) with the message that she will not come out to him again (if he does not pay). These are the ways of a prostitute acquiring money.

A prostitute should know from changes in the paramour's moods and facial expression when he has grown indifferent. These take among others, such forms as the following:

He pays her either less or more than he used to pay, or associates with her adversaries or acts contrary to his declared intention, or stops giving her the customary allowance, or forgets all about what he promised to give or backs out of it by giving it a different interpretation. or speaks in unintelligible codes or signs to his partisans in her presence or slips away from her on the pretext that he has some work to do for a friend, or speaks in private to friends and attendants of his former mistresses.

Before the paramour can, however, have an idea of the woman's intentions, she should take possession of his valuables on one pretext or another. A creditor (by previous arrangement) should take these away from her by force on the pretext of realising the amount lent to her to pay for expenses of the paramour. If he raises an objection, the creditor should take the case into the law court.

A paramour who has grown cold himself abandons the prostitute; it needs no special efforts on her part to evict him. If, however, the paramour remains attached to her but is no longer in a position to give her as much as he had given in the past, she should treat him with cold neglect as if he were an offender. If he should have lost his wealth and become unable to provide her any longer with wealth, she should take on another paramour and throw him out by the employment of suitable means. The external or objective ways of achieving this are as follows:

She indulges in what is disagreeable to him and persistently practises (in his presence) those actions that he thinks particularly reprehensible, sneering at him with her lips and stamping her feet on the ground. She spins out long talks with others on subjects about which he is ignorant expresses no wonder at his erudition or attainments in arts and sciences and, on the contrary, passes strictures on the shortcomings of his education. She tries to humiliate him by hook or by crook, passes a long time with men ranked above him, awaits neither his advice nor his assistance in her affairs, censures men having the same faults as he and remains in a solitary place (i.e., does not 'come out to meet him when he calls).

When the paramour approaches her with drinks, betels, etc. for sexual intercourse, she professes concern or rejects them, refuses to yield her mouth to him for a kiss, resists him in his attempt to gain access to her pudenda, resents his making marks on her body with the nails or teeth, creates a barrier against him with her arms when he attempts to embrace her, stiffens her limbs (so that he does not find her in an attitude favourable to coitus), puts her thighs one upon the other to prevent intromission by his membrum and pretends to be sleepy. She calls upon him to give her sexual satisfaction when she finds him fatigued, jeers at him if he does not succeed and has no praise for him if he succeeds. If the paramour, like a lust-smitten beast, tries to make up to her for copulation by day, she leaves the house and betakes herself to the place of a great man.

Further, she finds fault with whatever the paramour says and laughs when he speaks seriously. When he speaks Playfully she laughs as if at another's joke or looks angrily at and slaps, her own attendants. She interrupts his flow of words by launching into another topic in the midst Of his speech or recounts his shortcomings and vices, declaring them to be incurable. She gets her servants to say hurting words to him, avoids meeting him every time he calls and demands of him unattainable things. If even these fail to send him packing, she tells him in plain words that he is dismissed. All the above-mentioned observations regarding the acquisition of paramours by prostitutes have been made by Dattaka. There are two slokas in this connection: A prostitute should accept a paramour after careful examination. After acceptance she should please him; when he is infatuated with her she should suck him dry of his wealth and at last abandon him. This is the duty of a public woman. If a prostitute accepts these principles in remaining under the keeping of a paramour, no paramours can dupe her of her dues; on the contrary, it is she that makes heaps of money out of men."

CHAPTER 32
HOW A COURTESAN REPAIRS HER BROKEN RELATIONS WITH A FORMER PARAMOUR

WHEN the present paramour has been sucked dry of his wealth and thrown out, a prostitute should make up to a former paramour with whom relations were broken off provided the latter is still wealthy after having squandered a lot and is still enamoured of her. If however, he should have transferred his affection to a different woman, this will have to be ascertained. Such a former beau can belong to one of the following six categories:

1) He may have given up, of his own will, this prostitute as well as his next concubine.

(2) He may have been thrown from the house of this prostitute as well as from that of the next one to win attached himself.

(3) He may have left this prostitute of his own will but may have been evicted by the other one.

(4) He may have left this one of his free will and may be firmly established at the place of the other one.

(5) He may have been evicted by this one and may have left the other of his free will.

(6) He may have been evicted by this one but firmly established at the place of the other.

Of these six categories, the beau who has been evicted from both places (category no. 2) should not be considered for resumption of relationships though he may have made approaches through Pithamardas' and others. For fickle of mind as such a man is, he has no consideration for the merits or demerits of a woman. If, however, such a beau is steady of mind and wealth and has been evicted by the other courtesan who hoped to get from another paramour more money than he would give, he should be reconciled on the consideration that, being angry with the mistress who has just discarded him, he may lavish riches on the one who has sought reconciliation. If, however, he has been rejected by the other prostitute for being impoverished or miserly, he should not be selected.

Reconciliation with a beau who left her of his own accord but has been evicted by the other woman (3rd category) should be effected only if he pays excessively at the very beginning, but not otherwise. If a beau who left a prostitute and is well established in another place (4th category) sends out feelers for reconciliation, the pros and cons of the matter should be debated.

If she finds the position like this: "He had gone over from here to the other woman in search of livelier enjoyment and not finding it there. wishes to come back to me and wants to know if I am agreeable to accepting him again; if I do accept him now, he will surely give me riches out of love for me".; or like this: "Having discovered defects in that woman he finds many points of excellence in me ; in this case the appreciative beau will pile me handsomely with riches"; she should be reconciled to him, If, however, he is found to be in early youth (immature), or having a roving eye flitting from this woman to that i.e., fond of enjoying one woman today and another tomorrow), or intact upon cheating, or of passion evanescent like the stain left by turmeric, or whimsical even to the extent of doing injuries, he should not be accepted again.

If a beau who was evicted by the prostitute now desirous of reunion and who has left the other woman of his own accord (5th category) sends out "feelers?' for reconciliation, the first woman should debate the pros and cons of the matter. Should she find that the beau wants to come back to her out of love and will therefore give her much money, he being so enamoured of her qualities as to find no joy whatever in other women, she should be reunited to him. If, on the contrary, she has reason to suspect that he wishes to be revenged on her, by getting intimate with her now, for the mean way in which she had thrown him out in the past or that he wishes to regain from her, by creating her confidence or by acting as her willing servitor or by pretending to make love to her, the wealth she had cheated him of during their previous association, or that he wants to cause her to give up her present paramour and then to abandon her himself, she should conclude that such a man entertains no good intentions towards her and should not be accepted. One who has different intentions (i.e., is angry with her for having evicted him but harbours no malicious intentions) may be conquered in time.

The above procedure also explains what a prostitute should do when a lover evicted by her and established at another woman's place (6th category) negotiates for reunion through agents.

If a former lover, whether unattached or attached to another woman, now sends agents with an offer for reconciliation, a prostitute should take the initiative in me negotiations, though without giving up her present paramour, on one of the following considerations:

(1)that since he had been driven away by herself on the charge (real or faked) of making up to another woman and, having lost her, had gone over to another prostitute and is now trying to return to her;

(2) that as soon as talks with her begin, he would break off with the other woman;

(3) that her present paramour, who is vain of his munificence to her, should be humbled

(4) that he has stepped into a period of financial prosperity or has acquired or come into more landed properties or has

been appointed to a position of authority in the government;

(5) that he has lost his wife;

(6) that he has become a man of independent means;

(7) that he has separated from his father or brothers;

(8) that by adopting him again as paramour she may be enabled to get a very wealthy man who is attached to him in friendship;

(9) that by having him she may show her prowess to his wife who had insulted her;

(10)that by having him she may cause a rift between his friend, who covets his present mistress, and who hates her deeply: or, lastly,

(11) that by making a conquest of him for a second time she may increase the fickleness of his mind.

Having decided to take back a former lover, she should get Pithamardas and other helpers of hers to explain to him that she loved him deeply but that she was compelled, on account of her dependence to on her devil of a mother, to throw him out. a former lover also that she loathes her present paramour and hates his embraces. These persons, armed with some of the souvenirs presented by him to her, should persuade him to believe this by describing her past love for him. These souvenirs should be so selected as to recall to him memories of good offices done to, or evil prevented for, her in the past and indicate that she remembers him lovingly and gratefully. These are the ways of repairing a broken love. "

Regarding the relative merits of a new and a former lover, the earlier preceptors are of opinion that a former lover is to be preferred since his conduct and manner of loving being known, he is easier to please by the application of attentions and caresses. But Vatsyayana is of the opinion that a former lover, having been "bled" once here and then at another place, is unlikely to be able to give munificently and is, in addition, very difficult to be convinced of the love of the woman so as to be willing to give much, while a new lover can be easily entertained.

Each case, however, has to be considered on merits since all men differ from one another by nature,

There are some slokas in this connection:

Reconciliation with a former lover is desired by Prostitutes with the object of severing him from his present mistress or to humble the vanity of the present paramour. A deeply enamoured paramour is afraid of the prospect of his mistress uniting with another lover, connives at her faults and piles her with enormous riches out of fear of der leaving him. A prostitute should make up to one who is not attached to her (if he is liberal in spending) and neglect one who is attached to her (if he has been sucked dry); and when an intermediary of a prospective lover approaches her, should praise the paramour who is very generous with, though not much enamoured of, her. She should, however, meet and unite with her former lover, now approaching her through agents, at her leisure. In this manner should she retain her connection with her former lover without letting go the present paramour. After having satisfied her devoted and obliging paramour, a prostitute may go and meet another client and having milked' him of his money, come back and entertain the paramour over again. A prostitute should consider, first of all, her future welfare, then her gains and then the prospect of abounding love and friendship in reconciling herself to one of her former lovers."

CHAPTER 33
THE DIFFERENT KINDS OF GAIN

WHEN there is a large number of visitors and a large increase in the daily income a prostitute should not tie her of self to one paramour. She should fix her fees for the night on a careful consideration of the place, time, local customs, her own qualifications, her luck and her position in respect of other prostitutes in the locality. She should commission Procurers to keep in touch with prospective Visitors, and herself keep in touch with those connected with the former and belonging to her retinue. She should go in unto one man for two, three or even four nights in succession for the purposes of excessive profits and for those nights be have as if she had been solely reserved to him.

If, however, several visitors present themselves simultaneously and all of them bid to pay the same amount in fee but in different kinds, a should for obvious reasons distinguish in favour of the man who gives her those articles she desires most. Since gold cannot be claimed back (being unidentifiable) and is the basis of all transactions (the worth of gifts being assessed by their gold value), says Vatsyayana, the man who pays in gold should be preferred. Gold, silver, copper, brass, iron and utensils, cups, bowls, ornaments, etc., made of these, carpets, curtains, shawls, scarves, different varieties of apparel (silken, wollen or cotton), perfumes, spices, ghee, oils, paddy and cattle are the gifts to be considered in order of merit. Where the proffered gifts are all of a character not particularly desired or are all of the same category, one should prefer the article recommended by a friend or an will last long or be profitable in future. Other grounds of preference are merits of one visitor and liking for him.

Between a passionately attached and a naturally generous visitors, say the earlier preceptors, one should prefer the latter for evident reasons. But, says Vatsyayana, it is possible to induce generosity in an attached visitor; a loving man, even if he miserly by nature, can become very generous on account Of love. But, on the other hand, a naturally generous man does not give on account of the importunities of the other party. Even in respect of these two distinction should be made between the wealthy and the poor suitor and the wealthy one favored.

The earlier preceptors are of the opinion that between the generous man and the man who performs a good office of immediate moment the latter should for obvious reasons be preferred. But Vatsyayana says that the latter regards her as sufficiently paid once the good office is done, but a generous man never cares for his past munificence. Even in respect of these two the question of future prospects should decide the choice.

Between a man who remembers his past munificences and one naturally generous, the preceptors decide, for reasons stated to be obvious, in favour of the latter. But, says Vatsyayana, a naturally generous man, even if meticulously served for a long time by a prostitute, does not care for the wealth he lavished in the past on her? (and forsakes her) on the discovery of some cause of offence in her conduct or on an offence being imputed to her by a rival prostitute; for these men are often high-tempered, simple-minded and used to homage everywhere. But the other man takes into account all he did for her in the past is not quickly disaffected and, being of that turn of the mind which examines the qualities and faults of a person, does not believe in allegations falsely made. Even here, however, the choice should depend on the relative chances of future gains. The earlier preceptors opine that between a friends request and immediate gain of wealth the latter should for

Obvious reasons be preferred. But Vatsyayana says that while it is always open for one to earn wealth afterwards, a friend would be lost once his or her word is disregarded. Even here, however, the question of future gains should decide the choice. (Should it prove contrary to the friend's request) she should entreat the friend, by placing before her as a reason for immediate earning of money an impending costly affair, to excuse her for the day, assure the friend that the request would be honoured on the morrow and then accept the big money proffered.

According to the preceptors in a tie between earning of wealth and prevention of a loss of money, the former should be preferred. But Vatsyayana says that while wealth can be measured, a misfortune becomes immeasurable once it has started to befall. Even here, however, the relative importance of the two alternatives should decide the choice. This explains that the certain curing of an evil should be preferred to the doubtful acquisition of wealth.

Taking of money in such quantities as can bear the expenses involved in the construction of temples, water reservoirs and pleasure-gardens, the building of dams or bridges over lowlands, the furnishing of houses for consignment to the fire-god, the giving of thousands of kine to Brahmins through the intermediacy of other persons and endowments for permanent worships of, and offerings to, deities—these constitute the excess gains of superior courtesans (ganikas). The excess gains of beautiful body-sellers (rupajibis) of the superior type are denoted by ornaments on every part of the body, the building of big residences, and homes and furniture made shining with costly utensils and vases and a host of attendants.

The excess gains of prostitutes belonging to the superior type of the maid-servant class (kumbhadasi) are denoted by their ability to wear clean clothes, eat adequate food, use perfumes and eat betels every day and put on ornaments with a little gold in them.

The preceptors say that the excess gains of average and interior prostitutes of each of the above-mentioned categories should be worked out from what has been just said. Vatsyayana, however, says that these cannot be set down as invariable criteria for excess gains in view of the variable nature of a prostitute's earnings which depend on the place and the time and the prosperity, ability to pay and infatuation of the paramour and the sexual inclinations of the people of the locality.

A prostitute may forego considerations of cash gain and may accept small payment in cases where she

(1) wants to prevent the paramour from visiting some other woman,

(2) wants to seduce a beau attached to another woman,

(3) wants to prevent another woman from earning excess gains,

(4) wants to increase, by association with a particular beau, her own status, prosperity, reputation and attraction in the eyes of fashionable people,

(5) wants some visitor to help in rescuing her from difficulties,

(6) wants to discomfit a beau who was formerly infatuated with her but had transferred his affection to another woman by disregarding his generosity to her in in the past, or

(7) desires love alone out of the goodness of her heart. Should she desire, by attaching herself to a man, to gain in future or to avert a misfortune, she should take no payment at all from him.

A prostitute will, however, extract all the gain she can from a paramour when she thinks

(i) that she would forsake him and go out for a reconciliation with an old flame,

(ii) that he would go home and get reconciled to his wife,

(iii) that the head of the family next to him would control him, as with a goad, and prevent him from committing follies (like squandering on whores),

(iv) that his master or father would return home from a sojourn abroad,

(v) that he would soon be dismissed from his present position, or

(vi) that he is a fickle-minded man...

A prostitute will desire future gains from a paramour, whom she will please with all the appearance of devotion, when she thinks

(i) that the paramour being himself a noble, has promised payments which are, therefore, certain,

(ii) that he will soon have control over a State department or an estate,

(iii) that his emoluments are almost due (in the case of a State or private servant),

(iv) that his cargo ships or caravans are due to arrive soon in the case of a merchant),

(v) that the harvest in his estate will soon be ripe (in the case of a noble),

(vi) that her man always remembers services done to him, or

(vii) that he is always true to his word.

There are the following slokas:

"Avoid from a distance, in the present as well as for the future, those who earn their wealth by hard labour and those hard-hearted men who are favourites of kings. Go in with every care for those whom it is harmful to avoid and beneficial to keep on good terms with and make love to those on every possible pretext. Pursue even at your own expense those men of great enthusiasm and noble tastes who, when they are pleased, give unlimited wealth in return for small services".

CHAPTER 34
CONSIDERATION OF COMPLICATIONS AND DOUBTS ARISING FROM GAINS AND LOSSES, TYPES OF PROSTITUTES

In the process of amassing of wealth losses, complications with other objectives and doubts crop up. These arise out of deficiency of thinking power, excessive attachment to some person or excess of pride, duplicity, simplicity, trustfulness, irascibility, misjudgment or hastiness or out of bad luck. And they result in futility of the money spent (on catching a beau), future losses, suspension of payment of money almost in hand, squandering of money in hand, cruelty from others, non-recognition by intimates, bodily injury, cropping of locks, detention and loss of limbs. One should, therefore, desire from the very first to avoid the causes of these and disregard even those that may bring a lot of money together with these.

Wealth, religious merit and satisfaction of sensuous desires-these are the three desirable objectives; pecuniary loss, sin and non-satisfaction of desires--these are the three undesirable objectives. The incidence of one set of objectives (desirable or undesirable) in the process of pursuit of another set is called COMPLICATION (anubandha) or CO-INCIDENCE.

Doubt as to whether a certain action will yield any result is called PURE DOUBT (shuddha sainshaya). Doubt as to whether it will yield the desired result (i.e., where it is certain that some result will accrue but doubtful whether it will be the one desired or one of the undesirable trio) is called MIXED DOUBT (samkirna samshaya).

When a single action gives two collateral effects, it is called a TWOFOLD COMBINATION (ubhayatoyaga).

When a single action gives several collateral effects, it is called a MANIFOLD COMBINATION (samantatoyoga).

Illustrations of these will be furnished later.

The desirable trio of objectives are as have already been discussed. Those opposed to them are the undesirable trio.

The wealth received from a superior beau whose pursuit results in immediate receipt of money, estimation in the eyes of others, future benefits, association with men of merit and attractiveness is WEALTH WITH DESIRABLE COMPLICATIONS (arthanubandha). The wealth received from entertaining a beau without reference to his qualifications and only for immediate gains is called WEALTH WITHOUT COMPLICATIONS (niranubandha). Where an infatuated paramour is poor and pays by robbing another, acceptance of such money leads to an interruption of future welfare and to the dissipation of a prostitute's amassed wealth. Such wealth and the wealth received from disreputable or low-born visitors spoils one's future prospects and is called WEALTH WITH UNDESIRABLE COMPLICATIONS (anarthanubandha).

The pecuniary loss incurred by courting, at the prostitute's own expense, brave warriors, high State officials or miserly chiefs, which, though without effect at the time, is the means of prevention of troubles and of grounds of major financial losses and of increasing one's influence;. such loss is called LOSS WITH DESIRABLE COMPLICATIONS (arthanubandha). But the courting, at her own cost, of a deformed or ugly man who thinks himself beautiful or of a miser, ingrate or swindler proves ultimately unavailing. Money spent in such a manner is LOSS WITHOUT COMPLIICATIONS (niranubandha). Similarly unavailing is the courting, at her own expense, of a king's favourite and of an influential man of a cruel disposition, and since their ejection is attended with dangers, the money so spent IS LOSS WITH UNDESIRABLE COMPLICATIONS (anarthan bandha).

COMPLICATIONS of religion (dharma) and desire (kama) should be realised in the above-mentioned manner. MIXED COMPLICATIONS will be formed by permutations of the Desirable objectives with the Undesirable objectives, taking care to exclude those formed by the mutually contradictory objectives. So far about COMPLICATIONS.

The following are the cases of PURE DOUBT:

Doubt whether a visitor, though completely satisfied, would give her wealth is MONETARY DOUBT (artha-samshaya). Doubt as to the moral justification of giving up, on the grounds of not receiving money, a paramour who has already been sucked dry of all his wealth and who consequently is unable to pay any more is ETHICAL DOUBT (dharma-samshaya). Doubt whether, the desired man being unavailable, coitus with an attendant or an inferior man will lead to satisfaction of her desire is EROTIC DOUBT (kama-san shaya). Doubt whether an inferior man with influence at court, when refused by the prostitute, would try to harm her is DOUBT OF LOSS. Doubt whether the ejection of very much impoverished but attached paramour, who might go to the length of dying of the shock, would be sinful is DOUBT OF SIN (adharma-samshaya). Doubt whether the unavailability of the man for whom a prostitute may have conceived a strong erotic passion would result in her coming to dislike him is DOUBT OF HATRED (viduesha-samshaya).

The following are the types of MIXED DOUBT:

Doubt whether the giving of satisfaction to a new visitor of unknown character, who may be either a friend of a nobleman or himself a man of influence, would bring gain or loss; whether the giving of satisfaction to a practitioner of Vedic rites, a Brahmacharin, an initiate into holy orders, a man under a vow of periodic continuance or an ascetic, who has come to the point of wishing to die of love-sickness for a prostitute, in order to accede to a friend's request or out of pity, would be ethically justifiable or sinful; whether the reception, depending on hearsay reports alone, of a man whose merits and disqualifications have been neither personally or by others' testimony ascertained, would lead to the satisfaction of desire or to hatred—these are some types of MIXED DOUBTS (samkirna-samshaya), which may be further extended in number by crossing one with another.

Where a prostitute gains wealth both from a new paramour and the old infatuated paramour as the result of rivalry between them it is TWOFOLD GAIN (ubhayato-artha). Where union with a new paramour at her own expense brings no gains and the old paramour, being angry with her for some reason or other, at the same time, takes back his gifts it is TWOFOLD Loss (ubhayato-anartha). Where it is doubtful if union with a man would result in gain or loss and it is also doubtful if the old paramour would give out of rivalry it is TWOFOLD DOUBT OF GAIN (ubhayato-artha samshaya). Where it is doubted whether union with a new paramour may antagonise the old paramour and cause him to do harm to her and it is also doubted whether the new one, being angry with her, would take back his gifts, it is TWOFOLD DOUBT OF Loss (ubhayato-anartha-samshaya). These are the examples of TWOFOLD COMBINATION as given by Shwetaketu.

The disciples of Vabhrabya, however, hold that Two FOLD GAIN accrues where a prostitute gains wealth by uniting with a new paramour as well as without uniting with an old paramour, and that TWOFOLD Loss accrues where her expenses in entertaining a new paramour bring no returns while at the same time the old paramour, denied by his entertainment, causes unavoidable loss of wealth. Similarly, where no expenses are incurred in entertaining a new paramour but it is uncertain whether he will give anything or not and whether the old paramour, denied of entertainment will give anything, it is TWOFOLD DOUBT OF GAIN; and where union with a new paramour at her own expense leaves a doubt whether the old paramour, a wealthy man now antagonised, will again remain in her hands and also a doubt whether he (the latter). denied of entertainment will become angry and cause her harm, it is TWOFOLD DOUBT OF LOSS .

Examples of Twofold Combinations should in this manner of reasoning be cited by crossing and combining dharma and kama. So far about TWOFOLD COMBINA TIONS.

When a group of Bitas engage a single prostitute it is called GROUP CONCUBINAGE (gosthi-parigraha). This prostitute should cause a rivalry to grow among her paramours and by giving satisfaction to first this one and then another will extract money out of every one of the lovers. She should get mother to say to them, "Whoever amongst you fulfil such-and-such desire of mine on the occasion of the Spring Festival and other festive occasions will possess my daughter to-night," and should keep a watchful eye on the profits accruing from union with the Bitas as a result of such rivalries. This gives rise to MANIFOLD COMBINATIONS (samantato-yoga), which may be of the following six types:

(1) wealth from one or wealth from the rest;

(2) loss from one or loss from the rest;

(3) wealth half of them or wealth from all;

(4) loss from half of them or loss from all;

(5) wealth from all or loss from none; and

(6) loss from all and wealth from none.

Doubts of Gain and Loss should be deduced in the manner stated before, and so should those arising out of dharma and kama.

The following are the different types of prostitutes :

(i) The common whore (kumbha-dasi).

(ii) The attendant (paricharika).

(iii) The secret adulterers (kulata).

(iv) The open adulterers (swairini). ;

(v) The theatrical artiste (nati).

(vi) The woman artisan (silpakarika).

(vii) The deserter-wife (prakasha-binashta).

(viii) The beautiful body-seller (rupajibi).

(ix) The courtesan (ganika).

All these are subject to the same considerations of Paramours, their helpers, methods of entertainment, ways of earning wealth, ejection, reunion, special gains and complications and doubts of gain and loss.

In this matter there are two slokas:

Since there are ways in which men feel the need of sexual

satisfaction and also ways in which women feel the Same, and since this shastra is mainly devoted to a narration of those ways, it applies equally to women. There are women who passionately want love and there are also women who give preference to money. While the former have been dealt with previously, the latter have been dealt with in these chapters relating to prostitutes (Chapters 29-34).

CHAPTER 34
SECRET INSTRUCTIONS FOR BEAUTIFICATION, COMPELLING ANOTHER'S OBEDIENCE AND APHRODISIACS AND TONICS

THE principles of the Science of Love have already been laid down. Should one fail to attain one's objective by the processes detailed therein, one should resort to the measures being described in this and the following chapters.

Physical beauty, qualities, youth and generosity these are the four factors of good fortune in love. One may use the following recipes for enhancing one's beauty;

(1) An unguent made of tagara (valeriana wallichii) white kutha (costus root) and talishapatra (curculigo orchiodes) pasted together and smeared all over the body make one beautiful.

(2) The above ingredients are pasted finely and plied to the wick of a lamp which is later smeared with the oil of bibhitaka (belerica myrobalan). This wick is to be lighted and the soot arising therefrom caught on a human skull. This soot (koht), applied to the eyes, makes one attractive to women.

(3) The roots of punarnava (hogweed), sahadevi (vernonea cinerea), sariba (hemidesmus), and kurantaka (yellow amaranth) plants and the leaf of the blue lotus are to be boiled in sesamum oil, and the resultant unguent should be liberally rubbed all over the body.

(4) Garlands to which these ingredients in a powdered form have been applied are also worn.

(5) The stamen of the flowers of the white lotus, the blue lotus and the naga tree (calophyllum inophyllum), dried together, powdered and sucked with honey and ghee, makes one beautiful

(6) Smearing of the body with a paste made of the above three ingredients and tagara, talisha and tamala leaves (cassia tamala) taken together makes one beautiful.

(7) The eye of a peacock that has not shed its plume and that of a heat-maddened wolf, enclosed in a gold case and worn on the right arm on a day when the moon is in the Pushya asterism, make one beautiful in the eyes of women.

The following are methods of bettering one's luck:

The cocoon of a moth built on a northern bough of a badara (wild plum) tree and the rounded core of a Conch shell with a right-handed spiral, enclosed as above in a golden case and worn on the right arm in accordance with the rites prescribed in the Atharva Veda, enhance attractiveness.

One's fortune is also enhanced by adopting the special measures described in Tantra Shastra' and also in the following manner:

The husband of an "attendant woman' (parichavika) should keep her away from contact with other males. Thus kept back, she becomes an object of the earnest desire of a number of wealthy libertines. He shall then make her over to the man who pays the most in the competition to secure her.

A courtesan, when his daughter attains her youth, shall ceremoniously invite a number of wealthy men who match her (the daughter) in knowledge of the arts, dis position and beauty and say to them that the one among them that gives her this-and-this valuable articles shall have her hand in marriage. After this she shall protect the daughter from their contact. In the meantime, however, the young woman shall secretly, as if without the knowledge of her mother, be on terms of intimacy with youthful scions of wealthy citizens, meeting one or another of them by appointment during her lessons at the academy of fine arts or at the house of an ascetic woman or at similar places. The courtesan shall allow the man who pays as demanded by her to become the husband of the girl. If, however, the entire amount is not available from any one of the candidates, she should accept the highest offer, make up the deficit out of her own funds, and announce that that candidate has paid the whole amount called for. Or she may have the girl married in the daiva form and in this manner relieved of her virginity. Or she may get the girl united secretly to a beau, pretending her ignorance of the affair and then, as if surprised by the knowledge later on, complain to the court of justice and get heavy compensations from the lover. Or, as is the custom in the Eastern kingdoms, the courtesans may have her daughter's virginity deflowered by her women friends or attendants, give her a thorough training in the principles of sexual conduct (Kama-sutra) and those measures detailed therein that require constant exercise and, when she has become reputed for her beauty and glamour, launch her into the career of a prostitute. If given in marriage, however, the courtesan's daughter should not be with any other man than her husband for the space of one year; after that she may do as she likes. But even after the year is over, whenever the husband calls on her to spend the night with him, she must give up her gains for the night and come to him. This is how prostitutes are married". This is also a method of augmenting one's fortune.

The above also describes the manner of " marriage " of daughters of professional songstresses, actresses and dancing-women. Daughters should be given over to these who particularly benefit them in the matter of their professional activities or who please them best i.e., pay them satisfactorily).

Here ends the section relating to methods of increasing glamour and luck.

The following are the ways of fixing one's love on a particular man or woman:

(1) Sexual union after smearing the phallus with a Paste made by mixing the finely powdered seed of the datura (thorn apple) plant, black pepper and pippali (long pepper) in equal quantities with honey will make the woman fond of and obedient to a man.

(2) A powder made of teja (cassia obtusifoliam) leaves raised by the wind and caught with the left hand, remnants of garlands or garments on the chest of a corpse and the bones of a swallow applied to the head of a female and the feet of a male respectively, will cause each to love the applier.

(3) The powdered remains of the body of a she vulture that has died a natural death should be made into a paste with honey and ground amalak (emblic myrobalan) berry. This, smeared on the body before bathing, makes the woman he meets after bathing a slave to his love.

(4) The wood of the vajrasnuhi (euphorbia nerrifolia) and gandaka (acacia catechu) plants are cut into small chips and smeared with powdered red arsenic and pure sulphur.

This is repeated seven times. Then the wood is ground into powder, and mixed with honey; and the paste is applied to the phallus. Sexual union after this enslaves a woman's heart. If this powder is sprinkled on a fire at night, the moon viewed through the fumes will look golden.

(5) This powder, mixed with the dung of a monkey in heat and thrown on the body of a girl, will compel her to select the thrower for a husband (i.e., she will become so gone on him that she will marry him alone).

(6) A hole should be made at the fork of a simsapa (sissoo) tree, filled up with the extract of mango bark in oil and pieces of sliced bacha (acorus calamus) and cover ed over. The slices should be taken out after six months, made into a paste and rubbed on the body. This makes one beautiful like a god and enslaves the love of women, according to the preceptors.

(7) The heartwood of khadir (acacia catechu), sliced very fine, should be smeared with the extract of mango bark in oil, inserted in a hole made in the trunk of a flower tree and kept there for six months, after which It will have the same fragrance as the flowers of that tree. A paste made of this article gives beauty like a Gandharva (a mythical race of demigods) and is also stated to be a love-compeller.

(8) Slices of pippali roots' (long pepper) and tapara roots, smeared with the extract of mango bark in oil and kept in a hole of the trunk of a naga tree for six months gives beauty like a Naga (another mythical race of demin gods) and is also stated to be a love-compeller.

(9) The pulverised bone of a camel should be alternately steeped in the juice of bhringaraj (verbesina calendulacea) and dried successively for twenty-one times and calcined in a sealed vessel. This will produce a Pohl which, mixed with the kohl of Saubira (a principality in the Sind doab) in equal parts, triturated on a stone slab and applied to the eyes with a pencil made of a camel's bone, is beneficial to the eye and is reputed to be a love compeller too.?

(10) This also describes the kohl made of the bones of hawks, vultures, birds and peacocks, which also compels love.

The following are recipes for aphrodisiacs and tonics :

(i) Uchhata root (cyperus scariosus), charbya (choi pepper) and liquorice, boiled in milk with sugar added, should be drunk. This is an aphrodisiac.

(ii) Milk in which the testes of a goat or a ram have been boiled, should be drunk. This also is an aphrodisiac.

(ii) Milk in which vidari roots (ipomæa digitata), kshirika fruits (euphorbia pilulifera) and swayamgupta nuts (mucuna pruriens) have been boiled, taken with sugar, gives sexual vigour.

(iv) Milk in which the pulp of priyala (bacanania latifolia) seeds has been boiled and also milk in which sugarcane roots and vidari roots have been boiled give sexual vigour.

(v) Sringataka (trapa bispinosa), kaseru (cyperus esculentus) and liquorice pasted together with kshira kakoli (mimusops hexandra) and made into a pudding by boiling it with milk and sugar, if taken as required, will give such sexual vigour as to permit a man to enjoy numberless women, according to the preceptors.

(vi) Mashakamalini (phaseolus radiatus, a pulse), steeped in milk and half-fried in hot ghee and boiled in the milk of a cow with an old calf so as to make a thick soup should, when it is cold, be mixed with an overflowing quantity of honey and ghee and taken in as much quantity as required. This gives vigour enough to enjoy a large number of women,
(vii) Vidari, swayamgupta and sugar made into a dough with honey and ghee, should be mixed with wheaten flour, made into thin pancakes, and baked. Taken in such quantities as required, this will produce an effect as above.

(viii) Rice, smeared with the egg of the sparrow and dried— this being repeated thrice-should be cooked in milk into a thick custard. When cooled, this should be liberally mixed with honey and ghee, and, taken in such quantities as required, will produce such effect as stated above.

(ix) Dehusked sesamum seeds smeared with the egg of a sparrow and dried, and then mixed with sringataka, kaseru, swayamgupta seeds, wheaten flour and masha kamalini pulse, should be cooked into a mass in sugar and milk and afterwards fried in ghee over a slow fire. This should next be cooked in milk into a custard and taken as required, giving results as stated above.

(x) Take two palas each of cow's ghee, honey, sugar and liquorice, 2 tolas of grape juice, and 64 tolas of milk (25 oz.). Mix them and drink the concoction; this, called the "sixfold nectar", is recuperative, aphrodisiac, conducive of longevity and alterative according to the preceptors.

(xi) Mix the extracts of satavari (asparagus sarmen tosus) and gokshura (tribulus terrestris) with treacle and boil in thickened cow's milk and ghee. Later throw in powdered pippali and liquorice. A quantity of this to be taken every day, the course beginning on a day when the moon is in the Pushya asterism.

(xii) Take equal quantities of satavari, gokshura and sriparni (gamelina arborea) fruits, macerate them and boil them in four times of water. When only one-fourth of the water remains, strain the liquid.

(xii) Mix equal quantities of gokshura and barley. Take 2 palas of the recipé on rising every morning (ap proximately 62 oz.). This is stated to give results as in the foregoing.

Learn the special methods of causing and increasing love from experts in the medical science, the Veda', the Tantra Shastra and from experienced men in Atharva whom you may confide. Do not use those methods that may injure the body and those that involve the killing of creatures or the employment of unclean ingredients. Employ those methods alone that are not condemned by cultured and learned persons and are applauded by Brahmins and well-wishers as conducive welfare."

* Pala, in Hindu medicine, equals eight tolas (3.2 oz. approx).

CHAPTER 36
RECOVERY OF LOST PASSION: INCREASING PHYSICAL PROPORTIONS AND MISCELLANEOUS RECIPES

A MAN unable to relieve the passion of an intensely passionate woman should adopt special measures. He should preface coitus with the manipulation of the woman's vaginal canal with his middle and ring fingers joined together and when she nears her orgasm, introduce his phallus so that her orgasm precedes his ejaculation and she is completely satisfied. This is one way of satisfying a woman's passion. For a man of weak passion or an old or corpulent man with virility impaired on account of over-indulgence, fellatio is a means of restoring virility Or one may, whether of brief or incomplete tumescence or complete impotence, use artificial limbs shaped like a phallus. These artificial membra whether attached to one's Phallus or used separately, may, according to Vabhravya. be made of gold, silver, copper, iron, ivory, horn, tin or lead and should be smooth so as to give the feel of the living membrum, cool at the time of introduction and capable of standing vigorous action on account of its excitement-provoking nature. Some others, says Vatsyayana, prefer those made of wood.

The following are the different varieties of the artificial membrum:

(i) It may be a hollow body, the proportions of the inner side corresponding to the girth of the erect membrum and the outer surface being furnished with membra a large number of small nodules; this is to he worn on the membrum like a BANGLE.

(ii) Two bangles of the above proportions with three or four ridges on each are called a COUPLE (samghati).

(iii) Three such bangles, covering the entire length of the membrum, are called the BRACELET (chudaka).

(iv) A metal wire wrapped around the membrum to give it the required girth is called the SINGLE BRACELET (ekachudaka).

(v) A cylinder, furnished with holes on both walls of that end of it by which the membrum is inserted into it (for tying the line by which it is fixed to the hip and kept in position) and with raised, rough nodules on the outer surface to increase the woman's coital pleasure, and covering the entire membrum from tip to base, is called, if the tip end is closed, a SHEATH (kanchuka) and, if the tip end is open or latticed, a RETICULE (jalaka).

(vi) In the absence of these a tube may be made out of the rind of a bottle-gourd or from a reed or bamboo according to the size required, well seasoned in medicated oil and tied to the waist with thread. Or, the membrum may be wrapped round with a string of fine smooth beads or a number of rough beads like the stone of an amalaka (emblic myrobalan) to its base.

These are the methods of tying an artificial membrum. The use of these independently of, i.e., not as attached to, the membrum, is not customary.

In the Deccan there is the custom of perforation of the membrum like that of the lobes of children's ears. A young man perforates his penis with a membrum sharp instrument and as long as the wound bleeds stands in water. To prevent the perforation from healing up he engages in copulation several times at night until it hurts terribly. Then the wound is washed clean with astringent decoctions every alternate day and the size of the hole is increased by the gradual insertion of thicker and thicker wedges made of cane and kutaja wood (kurshi or Conessi). A paste made of liquorice and honey is applied to cleanse the hole which subsequently enlarged by the application of needles made of leaden foils, lubricated with the oil of bhallataka nuts (semecarpus anacardium). This is how perforation is made.

To the hole thus made artificial shapes of various forms and sizes may be attached to act as SHEATHS or RETICULES, such as: (1) hollow semi-circular sheaths, (ii) sheaths with a segmented bulge on one side, (iii) flat-topped cylindrical sheaths, (iv) elliptical sheaths like the petal of a lotus, (v) barbed sheaths, (vi) quadrangular sheaths like a crow's bones, (vii) sheaths shaped like an elephant's tusk, (viii) octagonal sheaths, (ix) sheaths furnished with wheels at the sides like a chariot, (2) triangular sheaths with projecting ends, and others of different sizes and for different functions and of a rough or smooth surface according to individual requirements.

As the membrum is brought to the required size by the addition of sheaths and rings, so methods are extant IOT procuring the enlargement of the size of the membrum itself.

(i) Varieties of insects that possess irritating hairs on their bodies are removed from the trees on which they How the size of grow. (mostly caterpillars) and vigorously membrum is in rubbed on the skin of the membrum, creased: perforation

which causes it to swell and be painful. It is then rubbed with oil to somewhat allay the pain and the swelling for ten successive nights, after which the insects are applied again, to be followed by rubbing with oil as before. When in this process there has been a considerable swelling of the membrum it is allowed to hang downwards through a hole in the bedstead to increase in length. When it has reached the required size, the pain is removed by the application of soothing extracts of herbs for a prolonged period, for otherwise the irritation would go on increasing. The swelling, called "brought about by insects", is resorted to by Bitas and lasts a lifetime.

(ii) If the membrum is massaged separately with the juice of each of the following, namely, asvagandha root (winter cherry), savara root (arthocnemum indicum) irritant aquatic weeds, vrihati fruit (solanum indicum), butter from buffalo's milk, hasti-karna (colocasia macrorrhiza) and vajraballi (vitis quadrangularis) leaves, there is an increase in size lasting a month.

(iii) Massaging it with oil in which the above ingredients have been boiled gives an increase in size lasting six months.

(iv) The oil obtained by boiling the seeds of pomegranate, cucumber. elabalu la perfume obtained from cerasus caproniana)

189

and the juice of the vrihati fruit over a slow fire, massaged or used as a liniment, also gives the same result.

The above-mentioned processes and also others for securing an increase in the size of the membrum be learnt from experts.

The following recipes are given for various purposes :

(1) If the powdered stalk of the vajrasnuhi (euphorbia nerrifolia) plant is mixed with powdered punarnava plant fæces of a monkey and langalika (gloriosa superba) plant and sprayed on the head of a woman, she will not desire any person other than the thrower.

(2) If one attempts copulation with a woman who has seared on her vulva a paste made by mixing juice of the ripe jambu (jambolina) fruits and of the leaves and bark of the vyadhi ghataka plant with pulverised stalk of the sona (ruta graveolens) creeper, abalguja seed, bhringaraj plant and upajihvika plant, one loses his tumescence at the very contact with it.

(3) The same result is obtained if one goes into a woman who has bathed after having smeared herself with a paste made by mixing pulverised gopalika, bahupadika (ficus bengalensis) and jihvika plants.

(4) Use of an unguent or a garland made with the flowers of the nipa (kadamba), amrataka (hog plum) and jambu (jambolina) plants causes one to be disliked in love.

(5) Plastering with ground fruit of the kokilaksha (hygrophila spinosa) plant causes the vaginal orifice of a she-elephant woman' to contract in one night.

(6) Application of a plaster made of powdered petala of the blue lotus. kadamba and the aromatic resin of 4 yellow sal plant enlarges the vaginal orifice of a doe woman' in one night.

(7) Application of grated amalaka alternately soaked and dried in the juice of the abalguja fruit and the aqueous

solution of ashes of snuhi, soma and arka (swallow wort) plants will cause the hair to turn white.

(8) Application to the hair of a lotion made with the juices of the roots of the madayanitika, kutajaka, anja nika (memecylon edule), girikarnika (clitoria terneata albus) and slakshaparni plants before bathing will cause the hair to turn black again.

(9) Massaging of the hair with oil in which the above ingredients have been cooked well also makes it black and brings the colour back gradually.

(10) If liquid lacquer is mixed seven times with the perspiration from the testes of a white horse and applied to red lips, they become white.

(11) Madayanitika etc. also have the same effect.

(12) A woman who hears the playing of a bamboo flute which has been washed and smeared with the juice of bahupadika, kutha, tagara, talisa, devadaru and vajrakandaka (synantherias sylveticus) plants becomes

(deodar) a slave to the love of the player.

(13) Food or drink mixed with datura fruits causes insanity.

(14) The use of old gur (treacle) brings back sanity in such a case.

(15) Any object touched with a hand smeared with the fæces of peacock that has eaten yellow and red arsenic becomes invisible.

(16) Water mixed with oil and the ashes of grass, will cause it to become the colour of milk.

(17)The paste of myrobalans, hog plums and shravanapriyanguka (aglaia roxburghiana) fruits, taken together, when applied to an iron pot, makes it look like copper.

(18) A lamp lighted on a wick made of cloth and discarded skin of a snake and soaked in the oil of shravanapriyanguka

fruits, makes long logs of wood placed it look like snakes.

(19) The drinking of the milk of a white cow that has a white calf is conducive to good fortune and longevity.

(20) Blessings from good Brahmins are also of the same effect.

CHAPTER 37
CONCLUSION

This Kama-sutra has been produced by carefully condensing the instructions of the earlier authorities and after following the actual sexual practice in different lands.

The person who has really understood the principles of this Science is in a position to pay due regard to the consideration of Religion (dharma), Wealth (artha) and Desire (kama), his own convictions and local usages and is not, therefore, moved simply by the urge of sexual passion.

The pictures drawn in course of the treatment of the different sections tend to induce, it is true, a heightening of the sexual passion; however, the application of the methods mentioned therein has been immediately afterwards censured and condemned.

There is no reason why a certain procedure or a certain technique must be followed because it has been described

In this Shastra; for the injunctions and instructions therein include all possible cases, while the application of them is limited to the considerations of individual requirements and feasibility in view of the time, the place and other immediate factors. The lessons of this book are meant for correct application in individual cases.

This Kama-sutra has been composed by Vatsyayana in the prescribed manner (i.e., truthfully and completely) after having received from his preceptor the proper interpretation of the principles formulated by Vabhravya and examined and verified them.

The principles laid down here are intended to ensure Social existence in perfect harmony and in pursuance of brahmacharya (a state of self-control and culture of the divine), and not to awaken or foment sexual desire.

One who has rightly understood the principles of this Science gains mastery over the sexual desire by pursuing without detriment the three objectives of life-dharm artha and kama and by establishing himself in the proper path for success in this and the next world.

Unfailing success awaits that wise and prudent man who, having learnt this Science, pays strict attention to dharma and artha and also has Desire without having excessive sexual passion, and who applies the of this Science in the appropriate manner.

APPENDIX
AUPARISHTAKA OR CONGRESSIO IN ORE

(This forms a chapter of the section of the Kama-sutra relating to sexual congress. Since, however, it concerns a frankly abnormal practice. we have lifted it out of order and put it for obvious reasons, in the appendix).

EUNUCHS are of two kinds, those disguised as males and those disguised as females. The latter imitate the dress, speech, gestures as well as the timidity, simplicity, delicacy and bashfulness of women. The acts that are done on the middle parts of women are done in the mouth of these eunuchs. This is called Auparishtaka. These eunuchs derive their pleasure and livelihood from this kind of congress, and live the life of courtesans. So much regarding eunuchs disguised as females.

Eunuchs who disguise themselves as males keep their desires secret. When they wish to do anything they lead the life of masseurs or shampooers. An eunuch of this kind, under the pretence of his professional duties, embraces and draws towards himself the thighs of the man he is attending to. He then touches his thigh-joints and the region about his buttocks. If he finds the membrum of his client in a state of tumescence, he presses it with his hands and chaffs him for the condition he is in. The eunuch then usually proceeds with the congress if his client, even if cognisant of the former's intention, keeps silent. If, on the other hand, the eunuch is ordered by the man to proceed, he demurs and at last agrees with difficulty (of course assumed).

The eunuch then goes through the following eight stages one after the other, namely:

(1) The nominal congress,

(2) Biting the sides,

(3) Pressing outside,

(4) Pressing inside,

(5) Kissing,

(6) Rubbing,

(7) Sucking the mango, and

(8) Swallowing up.

Stroking, scratching and other accessories may also be done during this kind of congress.

This is also practised by unchaste and wanton women, female attendants and serving maids, that is by those who are not married and get their livelihood by acting as masseuses.

The ancient and venerable authors are of opinion that Auparishtaka is the work of a dog and is not worthy of a man. It is a low practice and opposed to the orders of the Scriptures. Moreover, it is the man himself who suffers by bringing his membrum into contact with the mouths of eunuchs and women. Vatsyayana remarks, however, that the law prohibits this practice with married women only, but religious mandates do not affect those who resort to prostitutes.

The people of Eastern India do not resort to women who practise it, while the people of Ahichhatra resort to such women but do not indulge in fellatio. The people of Saketa practise every kind of congressio in ore with these women, while the people of Nagara practise every other thing except this. The inhabitants of Shurasenacountry (on the southern bank of the Jumna) do everything without hesitation, for in their opinion, women being naturally unclean, no one can be certain about their character, conduct, purity, practices, confidences or speech.

They are not to be abandoned on this account, however, because religious law, on the authority of which they are reckoned pure, lays down that the udder of the cow considered pure at the time of milking though the mouth of the cow and that of the calf are deemed unclean. Again a dog is clean when it seizes a deer in hunting though food touched by a dog is other wise very unclean. A bird is clean when it pecks at a fruit and causes it to fall but things eaten by birds are considered unclean. The mouth of a woman in a like way is clean for kissing and the like at the time of sexual congress. Vatsyayana further thinks that in all these things connected with love, every one should act accord ing to his own inclination and in conformity with the custom of his country.

Vatsyayana further says: "The male servants of some men practise fellatio with their masters. It is also resorted to by some citizens who know each other well among themselves. Some women of the harem, when amorously roused practise mutual cunnilinctus. Some men do likewise with women. The way of doing this kind of vulval osculation should be learnt from the mouth. When a man and woman lie down in an inverted order ie. with the head of the one towards the feet of the other and carry on a congress, it is called the "Congress of a cow".

"For the sake of such things prostitutes abandon men of good qualities, liberal and clever patrons, and attach themselves to low persons, such as slaves, elephant drivers and the like. Congress in ore should never be practised by a learned Brahmin, a minister of State or by a man of good reputation. Though the practice is not prohibited by the Shastras, that is no reason why it should be resorted to, except in a very few particular cases. For instance, the taste, the strength and the digestive qualities of dog-flesh are mentioned in the works of Ayurveda, but it does not follow therefore that the wise should par take of the flesh of dogs. In the same way there are persons, places and times with respect to which these practices can be made use of. A man should hence pay proper regard to the factors mentioned and to the particular practice which is to be carried out. He is further to consider whether it is agreeable to his nature and to himself.

After that he may or may not carry it out according to the exigencies of the circumstances. But after all, these things being done secretly, and the mind of man being fickle, it is not possible to ascertain what a particular person will do at a particular time and for a particular purpose."

THE END

Printed in the USA
CPSIA information can be obtained
at www.ICGtesting.com
LVHW021047220324
775219LV00016B/310